HELLO WORLD
THE NOVEL

HELLO WORLD
by Mado Nozaki

First published in Japan in 2019 by SHUEISHA Inc., Tokyo.
English edition published by arrangement with Shueisha Inc., Tokyo in care of Tohan Corporation, Tokyo.

Seven Seas press and purchase enquiries can be sent to Marketing Manager Lianne Sentar at press@gomanga.com. Information regarding the distribution and purchase of digital editions is available from Digital Manager CK Russell at digital@gomanga.com.

Follow Seven Seas Entertainment online at sevenseasentertainment.com.

TRANSLATION: Paul Cuneo
COPY EDITOR: Asha Bardon, Linda Lombardi
COVER DESIGN: Hanase Qi
INTERIOR LAYOUT & DESIGN: Sandy Tanaka
PROOFREADER: Meg van Huygen
LIGHT NOVEL EDITOR: Rebecca Scoble
PREPRESS TECHNICIAN: Rhiannon Rasmussen-Silverstein
PRODUCTION MANAGER: Lissa Pattillo
MANAGING EDITOR: Julie Davis
ASSOCIATE PUBLISHER: Adam Arnold
PUBLISHER: Jason DeAngelis

ISBN: 978-1-64827-558-6
Printed in Canada
First Printing: July 2021
10 9 8 7 6 5 4 3 2 1

HELLO WORLD
THE NOVEL

Written by
Mado Nozaki

Translation by
Paul Cuneo

Seven Seas Entertainment

TABLE OF CONTENTS

HELLO WORLD
THE NOVEL

PROLOGUE

KATAGAKI NAOMI CLOSED HIS EYES. Sinking into the darkness, he let his memories carry him away. He saw that night in vivid detail, projected like a movie on the inside of his eyelids.

The night was hot and sticky. The humid air of the Yamashiro Basin, combined with the July heat, made it feel like a sauna outside. Here and there, you could hear tourists loudly grumbling about how unbearable the weather was.

Naomi, however, had been born and raised here. To him, this was just what summer felt like—heat that stuck to your skin and windless, sweltering nights.

That was July in Kyoto for you.

Still, for Naomi, this was a special night. He was sweating much, much more than usual.

The reasons were obvious enough. First of all, there was the crowd. The Uji River Fireworks Festival was the largest in the prefecture, with an annual attendance of over twenty thousand people. The banks of the river were packed with spectators; the heat of all their bodies pressed close together was intense. You could practically see the steam rising from them. The stalls didn't help matters either. The sound of sizzling soba noodles surrounded him. The festival was in full swing. The night was alive with energy.

That was just *part* of the reason Naomi was sweating buckets.

Reaching back, he wiped the palm of his hand on the back of his pants. Unfortunately, they were so damp that a single swipe didn't accomplish much. He kept trying, and eventually his hand came away dry. But he couldn't bring himself to move it. He knew it would be just as sweaty again in a minute.

He was trying to hold hands with his girlfriend, after all.

It was their very first date.

She was the first girlfriend Naomi had ever had, and this was the first date he'd ever been on. He *needed* to hold her hand, in other words, but sweating all over her was out of the question.

Why didn't I bring a hand towel or something, damn it?!

He really, *really* didn't want to screw this up. But the more he thought about that, the tighter his chest grew. His imagination ran in overdrive, filling his mind with horrible worst-case scenarios.

In real life, sometimes you messed things up. Reality wasn't a neatly plotted story. In the books Naomi loved, exhilarating moments of anticipation inevitably led to satisfying, happy endings. But things weren't like that in the real world. In the real world, you could make stupid mistakes that cost you dearly.

That fear held him back. He'd taken her hand earlier, but he was too anxious to try it again. His fingers trembled uselessly in the air, frozen in place. After a moment, her fingers slipped through his.

Naomi looked over in surprise to find that she was already looking at him. Her cheeks were flushed from the heat; her sharp eyebrows were furrowed with determination. This had definitely been a big step forward for her. After a moment, she nodded, as if affirming her decision.

A sudden flash of light illuminated her face.

Naomi looked up just in time to see a huge firework blossom through the air. Its sound reached him an instant later, followed immediately by another burst of light. Brilliant colors filled the sky, and the smell of smoke grew thick in the swampy summer air.

He could feel his own heartbeat in his hand, pulsing against hers.

A particularly massive firework faded away, leaving the crowd to savor its aftermath. A round of applause broke out, marking a brief intermission. The crowd exhaled in unison as they waited for the next part of the show to begin.

In the gloom, Naomi turned to look at her. She was smiling happily, basking in the afterglow of the fireworks.

He thought his heart was going to burst.

In that moment, her smile became his most precious treasure.

Katagaki Naomi opened his eyes. All they could show him now was reality. Real life wasn't a neatly plotted story. Sometimes it took the things you love away from you for no reason at all.

Case in point: that girl was never going to smile at him again.

HELLO WORLD
THE NOVEL

CHAPTER ONE

1.

KATAGAKI NAOMI WAS THINKING about going to the bookstore.

The idea first crossed his mind on his way to school, as he walked along bus-clogged Shijo Street reading a paperback. He'd visited the store the day before, which meant there wouldn't be anything new for sale. But Naomi went nearly every day that he could. On the rare days he didn't, he often went to the library instead. Often, he'd visit both.

Since reading was his only real hobby, these visits were a part of his usual daily routine. The only times he consciously thought about going to a bookstore were when he had some special reason to do so, like when he wanted a specific kind of book he didn't usually read or when he felt like he *really* needed help.

Naomi rounded the corner at the Shijo-Horikawa intersection and Nishiki High School came into view. Just as he approached the crosswalk before the front gate, the walk signal started to blink.

He thought he had enough time to rush across the street, so

he decided to go for it. Unfortunately, the few seconds it took him to reach that conclusion made him wonder if it was too late to cross at this point.

As Naomi hesitated, two boys wearing the same school uniform sprinted right past him and across the street. Just as they reached the other side, the signal finally turned red. He could hear them shouting "Safe!" and laughing happily.

I should go to the bookstore today.

2.

THE CLASSROOM WAS FULL of cheerful voices that morning. After he entered, Naomi looked around for his seat. He'd only been a high schooler for a few days, so he wasn't used to his new spot yet. Actually, he *did* remember where his seat was, but he was always a little worried someone else might be sitting in it. This little ritual was his way of reassuring himself.

Naomi managed to walk over and take his seat without making a complete fool of himself. A group of guys next to him were already chattering about something. He kind of wanted to say hi, but they seemed to be enjoying themselves, so he was reluctant to butt into the conversation.

After a few moments, he gave up on the idea and opened his book instead. The story he'd been reading a few minutes earlier quickly pulled him right back in.

Once first period class was over, there was a brief free period. The guy in the next seat put away his textbook. He wasn't talking to anyone at the moment. This was the perfect chance.

But before Naomi could work up the nerve to say anything, someone else came over.

Oh, well. I guess my timing was off, Naomi thought as the two struck up a conversation. For lack of any better options, he opened his book again.

After second period, the guy in the next seat went off to visit a different class. With a shrug, Naomi went back to his book.

After third period, the guy in the next seat was reading a manga magazine. Naomi knew how engrossing that could be, so he didn't want to interrupt. He read his book instead.

When fourth period ended and it was time for lunch, the guy in the next seat joined up with a bunch of his friends to run off loudly toward the school store. The idea of buying food inside the building was still fresh and exciting to the first-year students, since that hadn't been an option back in middle school. Naomi wasn't about to blunder over and delay them. That would have been inconsiderate.

When he thought things through more carefully, though, he realized he hadn't brought a *bento* with him, which meant also needed to visit the school store.

By the time he finally got there, almost all the lunch breads were gone. There wasn't a single meat, fish, or cream-filled one left on the shelves, and the leftovers were a sad smattering of less-than-appetizing options. Naomi went for something called a "twisty bread," which turned out to be nothing more than a basic bread roll twisted into knots.

As he finished his meal, Naomi thought, *I should really go to the bookstore today.*

The moment the end-of-day homeroom period wrapped up, a hubbub of voices filled the classroom.

Naomi busied himself with packing up the books he'd be taking home tonight, trying to decide which bookstore to visit. His first choice was Oogaki Books near the corner of Shijo and Karasuma, followed by the nearby Kumazawa Bookstore. On second thought, Maruzen might have a better selection of the kind of books he wanted right now. If he headed in that direction, he'd also pass a Junkudo. Maybe the best plan was to hit up four or five places, one after the other...

"Hey, d'you want to come along?"

Naomi's heart nearly jumped out of his mouth. He spun around a little too fast, cringing like a child who'd just been screamed at. At some point, a group of ten-odd people had gathered right next to him. He had *no* idea what was going on. What had they just asked him? What were they even talking about?

"Sorry, uh..."

The girl who'd spoken to him hesitated awkwardly. After a few seconds, Naomi realized that she was waiting for his name. "Um, it's Katagaki."

"Right, right. Anyway, Katagaki-kun, we're gonna go hang

out and get to know each other. Thought we'd sing some karaoke, you know?"

Finally, the pieces fell into place. He'd been invited out with his classmates.

"Um... Well..."

Now that he knew the question, he had to figure out his answer.

Naomi wasn't a big fan of karaoke, honestly. He'd gone a couple times with his friends from middle school, but he'd been too shy to sing. And that was with people he knew and got along with. The idea of singing in front of people he'd just met was *terrifying*.

Maybe he wouldn't have to sing, though? They probably wouldn't force him. But if he kept refusing, that might get pretty embarrassing in its own way.

Also, there was the whole bookstore thing. He'd been planning that all day. But when he thought it through, the whole reason for that trip might be rendered meaningless if he just went to this karaoke thing instead.

So, there was no reason to turn them down. In fact, he *should* probably go, even if it did feel a little awkward. Naomi opened his mouth, his lips forming the word "*sure*."

"Oh, sorry. If you've got something else to do, don't worry about it."

"Um, okay."

"Let's go, guys!"

"Wait for me!"

Chattering amongst themselves, the group of students left their classroom behind. Naomi was left standing by himself, listening as the noises grew fainter.

I really need to go to the bookstore, he thought. *Right now.*

3.

OOGAKI BOOKS SHIJO was a store on the second floor of a building near the intersection of Shijo Street and Karasuma Street, about a ten-minute walk from Nishiki High.

A similar, brand-new building not far away was home to Oogaki Books Kyoto, the main branch, but Naomi had always preferred the smaller Shijo store. Compared to the Kyoto branch, where a whole corner of the first floor was devoted to magazines, this felt more like a proper *bookstore*—every inch of available space was *crammed* full of bookshelves.

Fortunately, he had lots of other options when he wanted some variety. That was the best part of going to a high school so close to the Shijo-Karasuma area.

Riding up to the second floor of the building on a narrow escalator, Naomi gazed out over a familiar scene. He'd lost track of how many times he'd visited this place, but the sight of it never got old. Near the front entrance, there were a few tables of notebooks, stationery, and new releases. But once you got past those, you entered a forest of bookshelves that stretched the entire length of the floor.

Oogaki Books was a chain local to the Kinki Region, with thirty-odd branches centered in the Kyoto area. Everyone living in the city was familiar with it; Naomi had been shocked to learn it wasn't a national brand. When a relative had told him, "They've got Maruzen and Junkudo in Tokyo, but no Oogaki Books," he hadn't believed her at first.

In all honesty, it was still hard to imagine living in a place without a single Oogaki store. Could you even call that living, really?

Passing by the stationery tables, Naomi glanced over the new releases, all of which he'd already perused yesterday. The sight was still kind of soothing—it felt a little like walking into his living room. This place wasn't *exactly* his home, but he still felt a lot more relaxed here than in the halls of his new high school.

Naomi stepped confidently forward into his natural habitat.

Glancing up at the signs hanging from the ceiling, he made his way deeper and deeper into the shelves. He already knew where to find the genres that he usually read—he tended to buy novels, manga, magazines, art books, and the occasional science book. But today he was looking for a kind of book he'd never been remotely interested in before.

Naomi took a right turn into the "Hobbies and Practical Skills" section.

The shelves here were divided by a thicket of smaller signs, each marking a specific genre. Naomi's eyes quickly focused on one sign in particular. The words on it seemed intense, even intimidating; just looking at them made him want to blush. But he screwed up his courage and approached.

For the first time, he laid eyes upon the "Self-Help" section.

At a glance, the titles were all alarmingly dramatic.

"The Harvard Thought Process: How to Win at Life"

"The Five-Minute-a-Day Millionaire"

"How to Shrug off Your Haters"

Naomi tensed as his eyes moved across the covers and spines of the books on display. They felt like a giant, invisible hand pressing down on him.

When he was in the fiction sections, even the most sensational titles never bothered him. Those books were *stories*, after all. He was just a reader who might enjoy them.

But these books were different. The books in this corner were purchased by people who wanted to change themselves in a specific way. When you brought one to the register, you were basically announcing that to the world.

What would the person behind the counter think? Would he look at the book and then at Naomi, stifling a laugh?

The thought made him want to melt into the ground. He was so embarrassed he was tempted to leave empty-handed.

And yet...

Naomi squeezed his slightly sweaty hands into fists. This was the whole reason he'd come here, wasn't it? He wanted to *get past* this feeling. He wanted to *overcome* his shyness.

Fifteen minutes later, Naomi finally reached out, grabbed a book with a paper band boasting 50,000 sales, and headed for the register.

Its title was *How to Be Decisive: A Better You by Tomorrow!*

4.

SITTING IN HIS BEDROOM, Naomi focused intently on his new book. His table lamp cast a warm glow on the pages, which made a pleasant whisper when they turned. There was no other sound.

If there was one word that defined him, it was *indecisive*.

He didn't know how long he'd been like this; it had just sort of turned out that way. Naomi agonized over every choice, even simple, harmless ones. The thought of choosing wrong, of screwing up horrifically, made him flinch in terror. He was the very picture of a coward.

To the best of his ability, Naomi avoided taking risks. He didn't like challenging himself unless the outcome was predictable.

He did enjoy studying, though. Put more effort in, and you'd reliably be rewarded for it. It was one of the few things he could focus on without getting anxious.

Naomi liked books, too. Reading them was a lot of fun, and moving steadily through their pages gave him a real sense of accomplishment.

Thanks to that, his grades had gotten steadily better, and he'd been accepted into one of the best high schools in the prefecture. *Careful* and *consistent* had been his watchwords all his life, and they'd served him well enough.

That wasn't to say that he *liked* his personality, though.

A part of him had always wanted to change, but he'd never found the spark to actually make it happen. He'd been waiting and waiting for the right moment to fall into his lap. On the day he entered high school, he'd thought, maybe this is my chance.

It wasn't like he wanted to completely redefine himself the way some kids did. He'd never even fantasized about transforming into some cool, popular guy who'd be the center of attention. But he did think it might be nice if he could change, at least a little. Maybe it'd make his high school experience more fun.

Surely that wasn't too much to hope for. He wasn't being overly ambitious here.

That was why Naomi had bought his new self-help book. In all honesty, he thought its 2000-yen price tag was kind of excessive. He'd never flinched at spending that much on a hardcover edition of a novel he enjoyed, but there was no telling if the advice in this book would be remotely useful. Buying it felt like a risk in itself.

He probably wouldn't have gambled his money on this back in middle school.

Maybe, he thought hopefully, *I've already changed a little bit.*

5.

THE NEXT DAY, Naomi sat in the classroom, intently reading his new book. Of course, the last thing he wanted was for any of his classmates to know he'd bought a book like this, so he'd put it in a thick, blank cover that hid the title.

Its pages were full of life-changing bits of advice in bold, eye-catching type.

"Don't overthink things! Make a conscious effort to decide quickly!"

At the end of fourth period, Naomi headed to the school store as fast as he could walk. He pushed his way forcefully through the chaotic crowd and made his way to the bread shelves. He'd made it here quickly; today, he had his pick.

His eyes found the barbecue bread, the most popular option. But the golden fish sandwich was also tempting. They both looked tasty, but he had to choose fast.

Naomi considered his options. They both looked good. Either was fine, really.

He reached out for the nearest barbecue bread, then paused. How much money did he have left in his wallet, anyway? He'd bought that book yesterday. He shouldn't buy too much, either. He didn't want to waste any food, or his cash.

By the time he worked his way through that thought process, the barbecue bread had vanished. The fish sandwiches and the three-color breads melted away like smoke, too.

Naomi just looked on, totally flustered, until the lady behind the counter finally shouted, "What's it gonna be, kid?!"

Naomi's plastic bag swayed slightly in his hand as he trudged back to his classroom. It contained two packaged "twisty breads."

He read his book as he walked along. Luckily, it contained a full eighty-seven pieces of advice, each designed to help you become more decisive. He'd decided to move on to the next item.

"Don't worry about what other people think. When you have something to say, speak up!"

When he stepped into his classroom, Naomi found that a group of girls had gathered, spreading out their lunches and packaged snacks across several desks. One of them was sitting in Naomi's chair. She'd pulled it away from his desk to sit with the others. If he wanted to eat his lunch here, he'd have to get it back.

Naomi studied the girl in question. She looked like a gentle, soft-spoken person. She'd probably give the chair back without any real fuss. There were plenty of other empty chairs in the classroom, after all.

Settling down onto one of the stone stairways that surrounded the main school building, Naomi took a bite of his twisty bread. It was nice out today, and it never hurt to get some fresh air. Or so he'd convinced himself.

Once again, he opened up his book.

"Don't let others do the deciding for you. Make your own choices!"

That made perfect sense. It was easy to nod in agreement. The tricky part was actually acting on that advice.

After finishing his bland lunch, Naomi headed back to his classroom.

Fifth period that day was a homeroom session rather than a class. Today, all the first-year classes were electing their representatives and officers. There was a long list of school committees on the blackboard. Everyone was expected to at least join a committee. The homeroom teacher led the discussion, helped by two students who'd been chosen as assistants since their names fell at the beginning of the alphabet.

Since they were all new here, most of the kids didn't have any strong preferences. The class worked its way down the list picking people more or less at random.

Naomi let it wash over him, lost in thought. He was murmuring inside his head like a mantra, *Make your own choices. Don't let others do the deciding for you.*

"Next up is the library committee," one of the student assistants called.

The homeroom teacher looked around the room. "Do we have any book lovers in this class?"

Instantly, a number of faces turned Naomi's way. A moment later, the rest of the class followed suit.

Naomi swallowed nervously.

Thinking about it...in his first ten days of high school, he'd spent most of his free time sitting in this classroom reading books. He hadn't done anything else, really.

The teacher looked down at his list of students. "Uh, Katagaki, right? How about it?"

"Um... Well..."

The words caught in Naomi's throat. They wanted an answer *now*. He could feel the anxiety welling up inside him.

It wasn't like he *disliked* the idea of working in the library. He loved books, after all. It was easily the most attractive option of anything listed on the blackboard. And yet, part of him *really* didn't want to say yes.

He'd been nominated for this by other people, just because everybody *looked* at him. He needed to make his own decisions from now on.

But he couldn't bring himself to come out and say that. There were too many sets of eyes on him. And the growing silence was too much to handle.

"Sure, I'll do it."

"All right, then. Katagaki it is."

Everyone finally looked away. The assistant wrote his name on the blackboard and moved along to the next entry on the list.

It had gone smoothly enough, in a way. But there was an ugly, muddy feeling lingering in Naomi's chest.

He wasn't even upset that he hadn't made his own decision.

He was disgusted by how *relieved* he felt to escape those eyes.

6.

THE FIRST MEETING OF THE LIBRARY COMMITTEE was held immediately after school that same day.

Students from all three years trickled into the special classroom where the meeting would be held, wandering around to find their seats. On a whiteboard near the far wall, someone had written "Welcome to the Library Committee!" in dry-erase marker.

Naomi had already taken his seat. Naturally, he was using this opportunity to read his book.

"When you're uncertain, trust your instincts!"

They sure made it *sound* simple.

Furrowing his brow, Naomi let out a quiet sigh. So far, this stuff was easier said than done.

Why do I have to be like this?

He'd made it into a good high school and earned himself a fresh start. He'd bought a self-help book. This was the perfect chance to overcome his weaknesses.

And yet, he couldn't even manage to buy the lunch he wanted. He couldn't even ask for his *own chair* back. Now, he'd been shoved onto this committee by his classmates. He thought he might enjoy the job itself, but he just knew that every single time he came here, he'd remember that he hadn't *decided* to join this committee.

He hadn't said, "I'd rather do something else, actually," at homeroom just now. And that fact was going to haunt him for a solid year.

Maybe it wasn't so easy for people to change.

"Wonder what class that girl's from..."

As he stared down resentfully at his book, Naomi overheard

the guys next to him whispering to each other. Following their gaze, he spotted a girl with big, round eyes. Her bangs formed a neat line across her forehead, and she had a ribbon in her hair—on one side, but not the other. It was a distinctive hairstyle, but it looked completely natural on her.

"She's like an idol, man," mumbled one of the boys a few seats over. Naomi silently agreed. The girl was petite and slender, and her smile was adorable. Judging from where she sat, she was probably a first year, just like him. But it looked like she was already on friendly terms with everyone sitting around her.

After watching her for a few moments, Naomi realized he was staring and looked away hurriedly. It wasn't like he'd done anything *bad*, but he somehow still managed to feel guilty.

The library committee chairman gave them a quick overview of their main responsibilities and yearly events, then wrapped things up early. The work itself *did* sound kind of fun, just as Naomi had expected. He'd always wanted to try sitting behind the lending desk at a library.

There was a chorus of scraping sounds as everyone rose from their chairs.

Naomi found himself glancing over at the girl he'd spotted earlier. He knew her name now, since they'd all introduced themselves. *Kadenokouji Misuzu* was a pretty striking name, but she was a pretty striking person, so it felt right.

A small group was already forming around Misuzu. Some

were first-year boys; others were older guys. They all had their cell phones out. They were probably asking for her contact info.

"Oh, right. One last thing, guys!" Everyone turned around—the third-year committee chairman was holding his cell phone up in the air. "We're gonna make a WiZ group for updates and stuff. Come on over here so I can add you."

Hurriedly taking out his own phone, Naomi started up the WiZ app. Fortunately, he already had it installed.

WiZ was the most popular chat app of the moment, and most people who owned a smartphone used it regularly. You could easily form big groups and send out notifications to everyone at once, so it was convenient for this sort of thing.

The members of the committee swarmed around the chairman. Once you had the app open on the Contact Exchange screen, you could easily add anyone nearby to your friends list, or join any open groups.

They'd already set up a group called *Nishiki High Library Committee*, and Naomi joined it easily enough. He breathed a small sigh of relief—the idea of messing this up somehow had given him some serious pangs of anxiety.

"If anybody couldn't join the group just now, just have someone else pass the messages to you, okay? That's it for today!"

With those words from the chairman, the committee members headed for the exit. It got congested right away. Figuring he might as well wait for them to clear out, Naomi looked down at his phone and checked out his new WiZ group once again.

Spotting the name *Kadenokouji Misuzu* on the list of members, he found himself smiling a little. Of course, he didn't have the nerve to send her a direct message. He could *never* contact her directly. Still, he felt lucky just to have the name of a girl that cute in his phone.

"Hm...?"

At that point, Naomi noticed something—or the *lack* of something, rather. Looking up from his screen, he glanced around the room. Most of the committee members had left by now, but there was one other first-year who also seemed to be waiting for the congestion to clear up.

It was a girl from his class. He knew her name already, and he'd just noticed it wasn't listed in the WiZ group.

The girl in question closed her bag like she was ready to head home. She straightened up and began striding for the door. She was about to leave.

But...

"If anybody couldn't join the group just now, just have someone else pass on the messages to you, okay?"

This might be a problem, right?

"Ich..." Naomi's voice came out softer than he expected it to—nerves, probably. "Ichigyou-san."

Ichigyou Ruri stopped in her tracks and looked over at him. She didn't smile or reply. Naomi forced a smile onto his face, but he had the feeling it looked kind of awkward. He needed to get straight to the point.

"Um, you...you didn't manage to join the WiZ group, right?

Maybe we should...add each other, or something..." The words came out slowly, in bits and pieces.

Despite being in the same class and on the same committee, this was the first time Naomi had ever spoken to Ruri. The two of them hadn't even walked here together from their classroom.

He'd managed to say what he needed to say, though. Now they could just add each other on the app and be on their way.

Ichigyou Ruri frowned slightly. A cold shiver ran down Naomi's spine. Had he screwed this up *already*? They'd be on the same committee for at least a year. Hopefully he hadn't somehow insulted her without meaning to.

Too nervous to say anything else, he waited anxiously for her reply.

Still frowning, she took a phone out of her bag and started tapping at its screen, using a bit more force than was strictly necessary. After a few hard taps, she paused to run her eyes back and forth across the screen for a while. It was hard to tell what exactly she was doing.

"Um, do you have WiZ installed?" Naomi finally asked.

There was no reply. Still silent, Ruri started hammering the power button on the side of her phone. The look on her face only got more intense. Naomi was tempted to run for the hills. She looked like she might start yelling at any moment.

"Nngh."

Naomi couldn't make sense of the sound at first, but he realized Ruri had let out a grunt of frustration. Pushing the phone back into her bag, she took out a paper and pen and quickly jotted something down. Then she held out the paper in Naomi's direction.

"If there's anything I need to know, contact me here."

Uncertainly, Naomi accepted the piece of paper. Before he could look at it, Ruri had turned around and stalked out of the room.

Naomi looked down at the note she'd handed him. It wasn't a WiZ username, or even a phone number for her house. It was her home address.

7.

THROUGH THE LARGE WINDOWS of the library, Naomi could hear the faint sounds of children playing outside. It was a pleasant background soundtrack for his reading.

The Kyoto City Library South Branch was located on Takeda-kaido Road, just a little south of Kyoto Station. The building was old, and it also housed a youth activity center, so the library itself wasn't especially spacious. Its collection was smaller than those of the other branches, and it only had sixteen seats in the reading area. But it was a cozy little place, and that was why Naomi loved it.

He flipped to the next page. There weren't many of them left; he was drawing close to the end of this story.

Today, he was working on a book by Jean M. Auel, an American author—one of the novels in her epic *Earth's Children* series, which is set thirty-five thousand years in the past. Its heroine is a Cro-Magnon girl named Ayla who was raised by a tribe of Neanderthals and eventually sets off on a long journey to find others of her own kind. There were six novels in all, and because of length, they'd been split into sixteen volumes when translated to Japanese. Naomi was about to finish off the very first one.

After reading the final sentence, he quietly closed the library book.

The children were still squealing outside. The world hadn't changed at all in the time he'd spent immersed in his book. But he could feel the story he'd just read slowly permeating through him from tip to toe. He *loved* moments like this.

Naomi basked in the afterglow for a few moments longer, then pulled a notebook out of his bag. This medium-sized journal contained nothing but his thoughts and impressions of all the books he'd read so far this year. He made one of these reading logs every year, starting back when he was in elementary school.

In one corner of the cover, he'd written down his current goal in small letters, "Yearly target: 200 books."

Flipping through the journal, he found the first blank page and wrote "Book #61" at its very top, then copied down the name and author of his latest conquest. Once these formalities were dispensed with, he jotted down his thoughts freely as they popped into his head.

Once he'd finally gotten everything out of his system, Naomi exhaled through his nose in satisfaction. Glancing over at the clock, he saw it wasn't yet 4:00.

The library wouldn't close until 7:30, so he still had plenty of time. And on the table in front of him, he had five more volumes of *Earth's Children* waiting.

Letting his momentum carry him forward, Naomi reached out for the second volume. But just as he did so, an announcement began to play over the library's speaker system.

"The library will be closing at 4:00 today for sorting of the shelves. If you'd like to borrow a book, please—"

Holding the books he'd checked out in his arms, Naomi regretfully stepped out of the library building. He'd been ejected from his reading spot at an awkward time in the afternoon.

Where to now?

Naomi's mother worked late, so dinner wouldn't be until 8:00 or so. That gave him four hours to kill. He *could* head straight back home and keep reading there, but the thought of that dampened his mood somewhat. He was in high school now, but he hadn't joined any extracurriculars. He didn't have any friends he could hang out with, either.

He'd been given that one golden chance, when his classmates invited him to karaoke, but he'd hesitated and missed out. And now he was right back where he'd started, reading books all alone.

Was it going to stay like this for the next three years? Was he *never* going to change?

He wanted to think that he could get better, but it felt disturbingly likely that he wouldn't. A cold wave of loneliness washed over him. He found himself yearning for a conversation with someone—anyone.

"Kaw!"

Naomi looked up, blinking with surprise.

For a moment, he'd thought he heard someone call to him from above. But it was a bird that had spoken, not a person—a black bird that slowly circled above the street. Its call made him think it was a crow, but on closer examination, it was hard to tell. The thing looked a little too unkempt and fluffy. Maybe it was an unusually *chubby* crow...?

As he pondered this, the bird drew slowly closer, and then dropped down to the ground right in front of him. Their eyes met.

Naomi felt a bit startled. Weren't wild animals supposed to be more wary than this? Was this thing going to attack him?

Then, he noticed something *very* peculiar.

"Wait, its legs..."

The bird had *three* of them.

Naomi blinked and looked again. He wasn't seeing things. This crow-like bird had a third leg positioned between and behind its other two, like a tripod. Was this thing a mutant or something? He remembered hearing that crows sometimes attacked people by kicking them in the head. If this thing went after him with those thick little legs, he'd probably get a nasty cut.

"Kaaaw!"

"Eek!"

Startled by the bird's sudden cry, Naomi dropped the books he was carrying to the ground.

Oh crap, I hope I didn't damage them...

As he bent down to check, the three-legged bird hopped over and grabbed one of his paperbacks in its beak.

"Hey!"

The bird flapped into the air and flew right off. Naomi stood there staring for a moment before snapping out of his daze.

"Hey! That's a *library* book!"

The bird was heading straight south down Takeda-kaido Road. Hurriedly picking up his other books, Naomi set off after it at a run.

Naomi's heart pounded. He breathed in gasps and felt like he'd run a good two kilometers already.

When he glanced up at the sky, he could see the bird in the distance, but he was certain he'd lose sight of it if he paused even for a moment. Gritting his teeth, he chased it down the street as it moved parallel to the Kamo River.

After a while, the bird abruptly changed course—it had been flying straight south, but now it flew off to the east. As Naomi followed it, he found himself dodging more and more people on the streets.

Finally, he came to a halt. In front of him were two neat lines of trees and a well-maintained stone path. The bird was heading for the hill this road led up to—a splash of green in the distance.

"It's going to Inari Shrine?" Naomi muttered disbelievingly.

For some reason, the bird was flying toward one of Kyoto's most famous tourist spots, the great Fushimi Inari shrine. Soon enough, it had disappeared beyond the tall *torii* gates standing in the distance.

Panicking all over again, Naomi rushed up the road, dodging tourists as he went.

The red *torii* seemed to go on forever.

Naomi found himself in the thousand-gate corridor of the Fushimi Inari shrine. He'd already passed the thousandth *torii*, which was located near the main shrine and labeled clearly. But the line of gates went on beyond it, stretching deep into the woods of Mount Inari. By now, Naomi was past even the rear shrine area; he was on a path that ran along a ridge, somewhere beyond the third and fourth crossroads.

The red gates flowed slowly by overhead, one by one, each much like the last. Naomi looked up between them as he walked, trying to catch a glimpse of that strange bird.

By this point, he was panting with exertion. He'd given up on running, but walking up the mountain was plenty of exercise in itself. He felt like his knees might give out on him if he relaxed for a moment.

After what felt like an eternity, Naomi stepped out from the tunnel of *torii* gates. Just ahead, another corridor of *torii* waited for him, but he paused in the small clearing, using the opportunity to look around.

While this was a popular tourist spot, there weren't many tourists who ventured all the way past the fourth crossroads. All he could see from his current vantage point was the natural landscape of the mountain—in other words, plants and dirt.

In front of him, all he could see was a long, unbroken chain of more red gates. When he turned around, however, he could see black characters carved into the back sides of the gates he'd already passed through. On their right pillar, there was the year and month the gate had been dedicated; on the left, there was the address and name of whoever had paid for its construction.

It's been a while since I came here last, hasn't it...?

Naomi dug back through his memories. The last time he'd been here was in middle school, when he'd come with some friends for the traditional New Year's shrine visit. They'd turned back *much* further down the mountain then. He didn't know if he'd ever come this far before.

He also found himself remembering what he knew about these gates. Their construction was paid for by special donations to the Fushimi Inari shrine, and there were two times when you were supposed to pay for one.

The first: when you had a wish you desperately wanted to have granted.

The second: when your dreams were realized.

Naomi stared back at the corridor of gates with a fresh sense of admiration. For every gate in this long tunnel, someone had wished desperately for something, or had a wish come true. That felt *really* impressive.

Maybe the atmosphere of this place was rubbing off on him. He found himself wanting to make a wish of his own. It was a bit audacious, considering he hadn't paid for a gate himself, but maybe the gods would give him a freebie if he kept things modest. Surely they wouldn't begrudge him finding that bird and getting back his library book?

Or maybe... Yeah, I know...

The sound of flapping wings interrupted Naomi's thoughts.

Looking up, he saw that the bird in question had perched on top of a nearby *torii*. There was no doubt that it was the same bird—that thick third leg was unmistakable, and it still had his book in its mouth.

Their eyes met. And just like that, the bird opened its beak. The library book tumbled down to the ground. Naomi sprinted over, picked it up, and looked it over for damage. It had a few minor scrapes here and there, but nothing too serious.

As he straightened up, he realized that the three-legged bird hadn't moved an inch. What was *wrong* with that thing? He felt like it was staring at him.

Naomi didn't expect to find any meaning in the behavior of a wild animal, but there was something very weird about this one. Maybe he should report it to some kind of agency? Or at least take a picture of it?

Naomi reached into his bag and pulled out his phone, then paused. With a glance around the area, he suddenly realized he was all alone.

He looked back at the corridor on the other side of the open area. It was empty, too. The tourists who'd been walking through it earlier had all disappeared at some point. Maybe they'd gone on ahead or turned back without him noticing. In any case, they were gone.

A small chill ran down his spine.

The air around him felt like it had gotten colder, or maybe

heavier. Right now, he was totally alone with this bizarre three-legged bird. He couldn't put his finger on it, but that felt...not great.

Naomi put a hand to his forehead.

There! What was that?

He'd *seen* something for a second. An unfamiliar image had flashed before his eyes—almost like a single frame of a movie, spliced in somewhere it didn't belong.

Again!

This was too weird. He couldn't make sense of it. Strange scenes kept popping up, only to vanish in the blink of an eye.

What was that just now? A notebook?

That one was some kind of ball or sphere.

Oh, now it's a bunch of torii *gates...*

"Waaaaah!"

All of a sudden, a person *tumbled* past Naomi from behind.

Startled, Naomi looked behind him. The corridor of *torii* was just as empty as before. When he turned back around, though, there was a person lying on the stone path, groaning in pain.

Once again, Naomi looked behind him.

Where did this guy come from? There hadn't been *anyone* on that path a minute ago.

Confused and unsettled, he studied the person on the ground. The voice had sounded like a man, but the hood of his jacket was covering most of his face, so it was hard to tell anything else about him.

The man put his hands on the ground and pushed himself slowly to his feet.

He was a head taller than Naomi. The jacket he was wearing was pure white and had a very distinctive design, like something you might see in a Paris fashion show. His pants and shoes were also a shade of white; together, they made the jacket look a little bit like a lab coat.

The hooded man began to stretch out and flex his fingers. After a few moments, he moved on to jiggling his legs and poking at his thighs.

"It worked," he murmured. "It finally worked. I'm in!"

For some reason, he sounded *triumphant*.

Frowning, Naomi backed away slowly. He couldn't begin to guess what this bizarre person was up to.

His confusion only grew when he saw the three-legged bird flap down from its perch to stand right in front of the strange man, resting its fat little legs on the stone path.

"Nice! Very nice!" said the man, sounding extremely pleased.

Naomi was really starting to freak out at this point. This was increasingly alarming stuff. Backing away slowly seemed like the smartest move.

The hooded man made a circle with his pointer finger and thumb and began to murmur to himself in a low voice. He hadn't even glanced in Naomi's direction. This was a golden chance to escape, in other words.

Gingerly, Naomi began to tiptoe off down the corridor.

He moved as carefully as he could, trying not to make a sound. He did everything he could not to stir the air. The last thing he wanted was to provoke some kind of a response. He had his library book back; there was no reason to hang around here any longer.

But then, just as he had managed to turn about 90 degrees—

"Hey, kid." The man called out to him. He was looking straight at Naomi. "What's the date today?"

It was a simple enough question, the sort of thing you might ask anyone you passed in the streets. Naomi decided it wasn't worth the risk of ignoring him.

"The... The sixteenth."

"Hm...?"

The hooded man hadn't waited for his answer. Instead, he'd mumbled over Naomi and turned away as he spoke. But a moment later, the strange man froze.

Naomi had the feeling that he'd just screwed up very, very badly.

The hooded man turned back to look at him. Naomi couldn't see the look in his eyes, since they were in shadow...but he could see his mouth.

The man was grinning happily.

"Katagaki...Naomi!"

8.

NAOMI RUSHED DESPERATELY down the stone path, going as fast as his legs would carry him. The path downhill twisted, and the stones were uneven in places. He felt like his calves were about to cramp and send him sprawling at any moment, but he didn't stop running.

Turning back, he saw the hooded man about a dozen meters back, chasing after him. The man was tall, and his legs were long. He hopped nimbly over the uneven stones and easily kept pace with Naomi's desperate sprinting.

Naomi was breathing heavily by now. He'd already spent a lot of time running uphill in pursuit of that bird, and now he was pushing himself again. His body wanted to collapse and rest, but he forced it onward by sheer willpower.

Why is this lunatic chasing me?! How does he know my name?!

The creepiness of it all made him shiver. There was a small part of him that really wanted an explanation, and a much larger part of him that wanted to stay *far away* from this guy forever.

He remembered the way the man had spoken to him earlier. His voice was powerful and arrogant, his words totally unconcerned with Naomi's feelings. Apart from everything else, this man was the kind of grown-up Naomi absolutely couldn't *stand.*

By now, he'd made it back to the rear shrine area. The hill was growing less steep and the path more neatly paved. There were a few tourists visible nearby as well. Naomi considered crying out to them for help but dismissed the idea reflexively. The reasons he'd done so only came to him a second later.

He was too scared to stop running, even for a moment. The man was very close to catching him now. And there was something else, too...

"Oh, right—"

It was the words that man had muttered earlier.

He didn't know exactly what they meant, of course. But he'd read a lot of novels in his life, and he had a gut feeling about what they *implied*.

Rushing down the path, Naomi finally passed under Fushimi Inari's towering Great *Torii*. He hesitated for a moment as he reached the little town outside the shrine, then bolted to the right. As he made his way through the streets, dodging both residents and tourists, his ears picked up the chiming of a bell up ahead: *ding, ding, ding*.

Yes! This is perfect!

Naomi took a sharp right turn at the next corner that he came to. Up ahead, he spotted the railway crossing that emitted the loud electronic chiming. Wringing out his last ounce of strength, he slipped under the crossing gates just as they fell and hurried into Fushimi Inari station on the Kyoto–Osaka line.

The next train was just pulling into the station. Naomi ran along at the same speed as the decelerating cars, then leapt inside the instant the doors slid open.

Close. Close! Close already!

After a moment, the doors slid shut and the train set off. Pressing himself to the window, Naomi looked outside, then ran over to the opposite window and looked out there as well.

There was no sign of the hooded man.

Did I lose him?

Naomi breathed a long, involuntary sigh of relief and finally allowed himself to relax. His heart was still pumping rapidly, straining to spread oxygen through his exhausted limbs.

After a moment, he noticed that everyone in the train car was staring at him dubiously. That was understandable. He'd just rushed in here like a man possessed, and he was still behaving strangely. Avoiding their gazes, Naomi turned to face the door and stared down at his feet. There was nothing he hated more than standing out like this.

What did I do to deserve this, anyway?

As the train passed over the Kamo River, he silently cursed that crazy hooded man.

A little while later, Naomi stepped up to the surface from the subway platform at Nijo Station.

The sun was already setting. He'd apparently spent most of the afternoon running around the mountains behind Fushimi Inari. He would be back in time for dinner, but that would probably be his only accomplishment today. At this point, he just wanted to get back home and rest.

Naomi hurried through the rotary area in front of the station, his pace still a bit faster than usual.

Now that he was back in his comfort zone, he finally felt composed enough to think through what had just happened to him.

Who was that man? Why did he know my name?

The man had recognized Naomi's face, so he must've known what he looked like. He'd been chasing Naomi *in particular*.

That might mean this wasn't over yet. Maybe the man would keep looking for him. He'd have to go the police, in that case.

Maybe I should go to them now, before it comes to that...

They might assign a police officer to guard him or something if he explained the situation. But that would really stand out, so he wasn't sure he liked the idea.

Honestly, why did this have to happen to—

Naomi stopped in his tracks.

It was a purely involuntary reaction. He'd just spotted something terrifying out of the corner of his eye.

"Hmm, very convenient," *someone* murmured. He turned toward the voice.

There was *someone* sitting just outside the JR Nijo Station, on a metal rail marked "No bicycles past this point."

It was the hooded man.

"Why..." The word slipped out of his mouth. Why? *Why* was the man here?

Countless questions spiraled through Naomi's mind. He'd taken the shortest possible route from Fushimi Inari to Nijo, right? Was there any possible way the man could have gotten ahead of his train?

Wouldn't he need to know *in advance* where Naomi was going? Did he know where Naomi lived?

Terrible thoughts came in quick succession, one after another.

The man rose to his feet. Ignoring Naomi completely for the moment, he made a circle with his pointer finger and thumb, then peered into it. It was the same strange gesture he'd made on the mountain. Naomi had no earthly idea what it was supposed to mean.

After a moment, the man broke the circle and turned his hidden face to Naomi.

A cold tingle ran down Naomi's spine. He couldn't help but flinch. His courage was near its breaking point, but he forced himself to stand strong. He was all right. There was no danger here. There were lots of people around—they were in front of a train station, after all. Someone would come running if he yelled for help.

And so, mustering all the determination he could, Naomi shouted at the strange man.

"S-stop following me! I'll call the cops!" His voice was forceful and *loud*.

An elementary-school boy wearing a yellow hat was staring at him with a look of terror on his face.

"Huh?"

Dumbfounded, Naomi looked down at the child. He could see his face just fine, but not the rest of his body.

The kid's face was *poking out* of the hooded man's torso. This didn't make any sense at all. How could one person walk right through another?

The boy recovered from his shock before Naomi did and scampered off, clearly fleeing for his life.

At the same time, Naomi noticed a number of heads turning toward him. The nearest pedestrians stared at him suspiciously. They'd just seen a high schooler yelling at a little kid for no apparent reason, after all.

Not a single one of them, however, so much as *glanced* at the hooded man. It was like the strange phenomenon just now had never happened.

Slowly, Naomi looked up at the man. His mind flashed back to the words he'd heard him mutter at the shrine.

"Oh, right. He can't see me..."

"Who...are you?" Naomi finally squeaked out.

"Don't worry, I'll tell you, whether you like it or not," he replied with a strong, confident voice—the voice of a grown man. "I'll tell you who I am. And while I'm at it..."

There was a smirk on his face.

"I'll tell you all about *yourself*, Katagaki Naomi."

9.

NAOMI OPENED HIS EYES.

The familiar wooden ceiling of his bedroom appeared before him.

The beams were faintly visible. His lights were off, but there was a bit of sunlight coming in through the curtains. The sounds of the outside world suggested that morning was well underway.

He rolled out of bed and looked around, not yet fully conscious.

Naomi's bedroom was a Japanese-style room with tatami floors. It contained some shelves—stuffed with two layers of books—and a desk, built into his closet, that held a desktop PC. On the walls, there were a few posters and a periodic table of the elements.

It was the same old room he'd been living in for years, and it hadn't changed a bit since yesterday. Naomi felt like he'd just awoken from some feverish nightmare.

Getting down from his bed onto the tatami floor, he savored the feeling of *reality* for a moment. And then, yawning, he headed over to the window and opened the curtains.

A three-legged bird was waiting for him, perched on the guardrail of his balcony. Naomi's face twitched with fear as he was pulled violently back into that nightmare.

The bird slowly spread its wings and flapped up into the air. And then, abruptly, it began to attack his window.

Tak tak tak tak tak tak tak

The window glass shivered with each *very* real impact. The bird battered at it with its thick, sturdy beak.

"Gah! Stop! Stop it!"

The thing didn't relent until Naomi finally gave up and let it inside.

A cool breeze was blowing. A big, beautiful blue sky stretched out above the large trees that lined the road.

Naomi was walking down Kamanza Street, around the midpoint between Nijo Castle and the Imperial Palace—in the center of Kyoto, in other words. He'd come straight here in his school uniform after the end of his half-length Saturday school session. It should have been a fifteen-minute walk from Nishiki High, but his reluctance had slowed him down so much that it had taken twice as long.

Naomi looked around as he trudged forward. This area was home to many public offices and official buildings, in particular the Kyoto Prefectural Office. It wasn't the sort of place a typical teenager spent much time in. A wide thoroughfare ran between two lines of beautiful trees; to either side, there were local streets that you could actually park on. This was the main avenue that led directly to the gates of the prefectural government's main building.

Naomi turned his attention to the sky for a moment.

That damn bird was still up there, circling above him endlessly. It was both a guide and an observer, here to make sure he went straight to his destination and didn't try to run for it.

Naomi let his gaze fall back to street level and tried to focus on what was right ahead of him. There was an imposing Western-style mansion just across the road, the former main office of the Kyoto government. It was a historic building dating back to year 37 of the Meiji era, officially designated as a culturally significant structure, but even now, parts of it were occupied by certain sections of the government. It was the single oldest public office in Japan still in active use.

The hooded man was standing in front of its main gate.

Grimacing, Naomi forced himself to pick up the pace. He was too intimidated by the man to make it obvious how reluctant he was about all of this.

Making his way over the crosswalk, he approached his waiting tormentor.

"Well, I see you made it here, at least," the man called out casually. He was dressed the same as yesterday—in his fashionable protective coat, with the hood pulled down over his face. Unfortunately, he hadn't gotten any less sketchy looking overnight.

"It's not like I had much choice," Naomi muttered sulkily. It was all the defiance he could muster.

"Don't be such a whiner, kid. It's not like you had anything else to do."

"How would you know?" Naomi said. "I've got all sorts of stuff to do on the weekends, actually."

"Still working on those two hundred books, huh?"

Naomi jerked in surprise, but the man was already striding onto the grounds of the old government building. He had no choice but to hurry after him.

The floor inside the building shone like a mirror.

In between pieces of modern interior décor, there were Japanese-style wooden accents; the design was a striking mixture of traditional and futuristic. Naomi looked around the place with some interest. It was the first time he'd ever been in here.

A tag with the word *Visitor* printed on it in bold letters hung around his neck.

The hooded man had guided Naomi to a specific facility inside the spacious building—the Chronicle Kyoto Project Center. Naomi had heard the name mentioned before, but he had no idea what they actually did here. He hadn't even known they gave tours to the public.

A huge decorative wooden lattice panel some ten meters in length caught Naomi's eye for a long moment. It was probably supposed to represent traditional Kyoto-style design, but in all honesty, it seemed more like an attempt to show off how much money they had to throw around in here.

This facility was located in the basement of the old government building, so Naomi hadn't been expecting anything quite this grand and showy. The name Chronicle Kyoto had evoked something like an old warehouse full of dusty ancient books. This place was nothing like what he'd pictured.

Glancing around, he spotted a large Pluura logo on one wall, and had to re-evaluate his assessment of this place once again. Apparently, this was the sort of project that could attract an investment from one of the biggest companies in the world.

There probably wasn't a single person on the planet who hadn't heard of Pluura, the biggest web services company in existence. Their search site was simply Pluura, their email service was P-Mail, their mapping service was Pluura Maps, and their game store was Pluura Play. If you spent any time on the internet at all, it was basically impossible to avoid interacting with their products.

Naomi didn't have any personal connection to the company, but it was such a familiar part of his life that he felt a little more comfortable than he did before.

"Please gather over here, everyone!" called the woman who would be leading the tour.

Once the ten-odd people in their group had gathered around

her, an explanatory video started playing on a huge monitor mounted on the wall.

Naomi glanced to his side. The hooded man was standing there next to him. Another visitor was right behind him, looking straight toward the monitor.

He really is invisible, huh...

The hooded man was tall, and the visitor behind him was a short woman. She was looking right into his back, in other words. But instead of complaining or moving over, she just stared forward with a look of interest on her face. She was obviously seeing right through him.

It was hard to understand. To Naomi, the man looked absolutely real. There wasn't any fuzziness to him, like you'd see on a hologram; he wasn't even partially transparent.

Naomi hadn't tried actually touching him yet, though. He thought that might make him angry.

He'd read stories like this before, of course. He'd seen similar things in movies and on TV. It wasn't that unusual for a mysterious being to appear to the protagonist while remaining invisible to everyone else. A visit like that typically kicked off some sort of adventure.

But now that he was living that very scenario, Naomi wasn't feeling any of the thrilled anticipation he experienced when starting a new novel. Instead, he felt intensely anxious and profoundly weirded out.

It was simple enough, really. He just wasn't cut out to be a protagonist.

He'd read a *lot* of books, but he couldn't remember a single hero who bought self-help books to boost his confidence, only to continue being extremely awkward.

Apparently noticing Naomi's gaze, the hooded man looked over at him. Naomi hurriedly turned his attention back to the guide.

"Seven years ago, Pluura partnered with Kyoto College and the city government to launch a joint project."

Two bold words appeared on the screen. "That project is *Chronicle Kyoto*."

The monitor immediately switched over to a map of the city. It was the typical Pluura Maps overhead view, just as it appeared on a smartphone screen.

"I expect you're all familiar with Pluura's primary areas of business. The company provides email, maps, and many other convenient web services. We've come to rely heavily on them in many facets of our lives."

The map on the screen suddenly tilted to one side, and the buildings and geographical features took on real depth. It was a 3D map of the city—another of Pluura Maps' familiar functions.

"One of their main services, Pluura Maps, is widely considered the world's most advanced geographic information system. It's a continually updated record of the entire surface of our planet. From the world's cities to its wildest corners, Pluura gathers images and measurements at ground level, from satellites, and even from low-altitude drones. They provide high-resolution maps, updated on a *daily* basis, to everyone who uses their service."

The 3D map on the screen zoomed in rapidly until they were *inside* a commercial building. As long as the owner gave their permission, Pluura Maps could show you interior images as well.

"Pluura isn't resting on their laurels, however. They're actively developing new, exciting improvements to their mapping service. And one of those projects..." The camera zoomed in even closer, taking them from the inside of the building, to the inside of one specific store, then inside a specific showcase in that store, until a single pastry filled the entire screen. "...was the pursuit of *ultra* HD imaging within a specific urban area."

The guide had emphasized that last sentence a bit. Maybe it was a line they really wanted you to remember.

"It just so happens that Kyoto, this very city, was chosen as the pilot participant for this initiative. It's a city with a long, rich history, and it's home to more *intact* works of culturally significant architecture than any other place on Earth. This made it an ideal candidate for thorough, top-to-bottom mapping. In addition, its location in a valley offered an easy boundary for the project area. And so, seven years ago, the Kyoto municipal government reached an agreement with Pluura—and its partner, Kyoto College—to launch this project."

The pastry began to shrink as the camera zoomed back out. In seconds, they were outside of the building entirely, and soon the screen was once again displaying the entire city. But this time, the 3D map of Kyoto began to change.

A house suddenly crumbled and disappeared, replaced by a vacant lot. An instant later, the site was filled with construction equipment; just as quickly, an apartment building was standing there.

It took a few moments for Naomi to understand what he was seeing. It was a time-lapse depiction of a changing Kyoto.

New houses sprung up here and there. Shops appeared. Roads moved around.

"The goal was to map Kyoto far more accurately, and in far more detail, than ever before. And also, crucially, to preserve a *historical record* of all this information—a record of all the city's changes through the years."

The city finally stopped shifting around, and today's date appeared on the screen. Apparently it was now displaying the Kyoto of the present.

The tour guide held out her hand to indicate the map. "And that, ladies and gentlemen, is what Chronicle Kyoto is all about."

"Or so the official story goes," the hooded man said.

So, the others couldn't *hear* him, either.

Ushered onward by the guide, the tour group proceeded further into the facility. There were signs and explanation panels all over the place. It was clear this facility had been designed with visitors in mind.

As they continued down the hallway, they came to a large glass-walled room on their left. There was a sign that just read LABORATORY above the door; the people working inside were wearing uniforms of some kind. Naomi watched them as he walked along, wondering idly what they were researching in there.

At that point, a door inside the room slid open and a weird old guy emerged.

Naomi frowned dubiously; the words *weird old guy* really did feel like the only appropriate description. The man was wearing a T-shirt, shorts, and sneakers—a pretty casual outfit for a middle-aged guy, even if you ignored the cartoony Eizan Electric mascot on the T-shirt. And then there were the two plastic tulips that appeared to be sprouting from his head like the horns of some Star Trek alien.

Weird pretty much summed it up.

The odd man started using a small toy drone, and soon had it divebombing the people who were hard at work inside the laboratory. A beautiful woman appeared to be shouting at him, but he didn't seem inclined to stop. The glass walls muffled their voices completely; it was kind of like watching a slapstick silent movie.

Suddenly, the weird guy turned toward Naomi, and their eyes met. The man stuck out his tongue, threw up peace signs with both his hands, and began to dance. Finally reaching the limit of his endurance, Naomi looked away and hurried off. He didn't want someone like that remembering his face.

When he glanced over, though, he noticed that the hooded man was smiling. Was that his idea of comedy? It was just one more thing they weren't on the same page about.

A few minutes later, Naomi was staring through a glass wall at an enormous sphere.

The thing had to be four or five meters tall, and only the top half of it was visible—its total diameter was probably closer to ten meters.

The group had reached the final room of their tour, according to the map on their pamphlet. Inside it, they'd found this huge white ball enshrined behind a cylinder of glass, its lower half buried in the floor.

The word *AllTale* was engraved in English on the sphere's surface. That didn't mean much to Naomi, though.

"As I'm sure you might imagine, continually recording the state of an entire city requires an impossibly massive amount of storage space," the guide said, her voice echoing against the walls. "However, Pluura's advances in quantum computing, in combination with some cutting-edge research from Kyoto College, made this possible. What you're looking at is the fruit of multiple technological breakthroughs: it's a storage device that *never* runs out of space."

The guide paused for a moment to gesture dramatically at the object behind the glass.

"We call it AllTale—the world's first quantum storage device."

Hmm, wait. That actually sounds kind of familiar...

Naomi couldn't put his finger on it, but he thought he might have heard or seen the word AllTale before. Maybe it was in some science article he'd skimmed a while ago?

But even aside from that vague memory...there was something about this spherical device itself that felt very familiar. He almost felt like he'd seen it before.

Wait... Yeah, that's right!

It came to him after a moment—he'd seen this thing in one of the images that flashed before his eyes back at Fushimi Inari shrine. Or something like it, at least.

What were those images, anyway? I don't get it...

"Let's go."

Naomi turned toward the sound of the voice. The hooded man had already stepped away from the tour group and was striding along casually in the direction from which they'd come.

"Hey! Wa—"

The tour guide had already launched right into a new explanation of something or other. Flustered, Naomi looked from her to the hooded man and back again.

"Um, sorry! I, uh, I have to leave now!"

Bowing his head a few times to tour group, he set off after the hooded man at a trot. He *knew* a couple people were shooting him weird looks, and it made him blush.

As he hurried along, he muttered a few choice words to his invisible tormentor—in the safety of his own mind.

10.

THE FOREST WITHIN the Imperial Palace grounds sped by outside the window.

As instructed by the hooded man, Naomi had caught a city

bus heading down Imadegawa Street. It was afternoon now, so things were relatively crowded. He held onto a strap with one hand and gripped his cell phone in the other.

At the moment, he was looking at the Pluura Maps app. A blue line showed the path to the destination the man had specified, marked with a pin and the word *Demachiyanagi*.

Naomi tapped the screen. The camera zoomed in, changing from a map to street-level photographs of the area. It was a fully rotatable 360-degree image, complete with pedestrians frozen in mid-stride.

"So Chronicle Kyoto is just a much more detailed version of this, right?" he asked.

The hooded man stood calmly at his side. He wasn't bothering to hold on to anything, even for show.

"In a sense, yes. But there's really no comparison," he replied. "As a quantum storage device, AllTale has infinite capacity. We're not talking about twice as much storage space, or even ten times as much. It can record billions or trillions of times more information than any conventional computer system."

"Those numbers are so large, it's kind of hard to actually grasp..."

"Ahem."

Naomi looked over his shoulder. A middle-aged man in a suit was staring at him with an annoyed expression on his face. Naomi realized he'd been talking to "himself" fairly loudly.

The man in the hood snorted in amusement. Somehow, Naomi managed to hate him just a little bit more.

After a while, the bus pulled into the stop outside Demachiyanagi Station. As soon as they disembarked, the hooded man walked off quickly.

"Get a move on. We're cutting it close."

Totally bewildered, Naomi hurried after him. It was hard to keep up with his long-legged strides; Naomi had to jog along, in fact. It felt like the man was rubbing his height in his face or something.

Out of spite, Naomi picked up the pace until he was walking alongside the hooded man.

"You were looking at Map View mode earlier, right?" the man said.

"Huh? Oh. Yeah."

"There were pedestrians in the images, weren't there?"

"Sure."

"Here's a question for you," the man said, his tone dropping lower than usual. "Do you think the people in those photos *know* they're inside a photo?"

Naomi furrowed his brow at that. The question didn't make much sense. Even after turning it over in his mind, it still seemed nonsensical.

As he hesitated over his reply, the two of them arrived at their destination. The hooded man hopped down off the sidewalk, then ran down the embankment leading to the river.

They'd come to the Kamo Delta, a triangular piece of land where the Kamo River meets the Takano. There were stepping stones leading from the top of the triangle to either side, so you could get from one side to the other on foot. It was a famous local spot that got featured in a lot of movies and TV shows.

Naomi and the hooded man were on the east side of the delta, on a paved section of the Takano riverbank. It was still early afternoon, and there were tourists nearby, lounging in the grass or hopping their way across the river.

In the sky above them, one of the mapping drones Naomi had just heard so much about was circling quietly. The faint humming of its propellers only accentuated the peacefulness of the moment.

That was the only thing of interest he could see.

Naomi blinked in confusion. "Uh, there's nothing here..." They'd rushed over in a big hurry, but from what he could tell, there wasn't anything special going on.

"Wrong. There's something here, all right," the hooded man said, turning back to face Naomi. The two of them stared at each other in silence for a long moment. Finally, the hooded man smirked.

"Specifically, a prerecorded event."

Naomi frowned. *What's that supposed to mean?*

In that same moment—he saw something moving out of the corner of his eye. Turning toward it reflexively, he realized it was a small shadow darting across the ground. He looked up to find the source.

Something up there was falling toward him.

"Gah!"

He had no chance to react in time. A blow to the head

staggered him; the next thing he knew, he was down on the ground on all fours, staring at the concrete in a daze.

Two drops of blood dripped to the ground before his eyes.

After a long moment, his brain finally started functioning again. Something had just fallen from the sky and hit him. He'd seen a glimpse of a propeller.

Was that the drone?

"Let me take you back to the year 2020." The hooded man said. "That was when the *real* Chronicle Kyoto project began, operating under the utmost secrecy."

The hooded man walked up and paused in front of the fallen drone. The thing's propeller was damaged; a small light flashed on its body to indicate potential danger. The man stared down at it for a moment.

"The plan was to use a huge network of surveillance and measurement machines to precisely monitor the entire city, recording all detectable phenomena in AllTale."

"What?" Naomi asked, dazed. Pressing a hand to his forehead, he looked up. He could feel a trickle of liquid against his palm.

"All...*what*?"

"Jumping forward to April 17th, 2027," the man continued, ignoring Naomi entirely as he listed today's date, "Katagaki Naomi, attempting to read a book on the riverbank, was hit by a malfunctioning drone that fell from the sky. This left him with a nasty cut on his forehead."

He paused for a moment to point at the drone.

"That's the past, as recorded in AllTale."

"The past?" Naomi parroted back numbly. It took a moment for the meaning of the word to work its way into his mind.

"Yes." The hooded man didn't seem inclined to give Naomi's brain a chance to catch up. With a sweeping gesture of his arm, he indicated the city as a whole. "This is a record of Kyoto, as it existed in the past." Next, he pointed down at Naomi where he crouched on the ground. "And you are a record of Katagaki Naomi as *he* existed in the past."

"Uh, I..."

Slowly, Naomi began to make sense of this. The strange question the man had asked a few minutes earlier seemed much more relevant now.

Do you think the people in those photos know they're inside a photo?

Those people in the Map View weren't real. They were just images. Data.

Records of the past.

"I'm...a *record*?"

The man nodded firmly. "That's correct. And as for me..." He reached up to the hood he always wore. Slowly, he began to pull it back.

Little by little, his face came into view. His cheeks looked a little thin, and there were bags under his eyes.

"I'm a man who's accessing the AllTale system from the real world, in the year 2037." Finally, he yanked the hood back completely. The man looked like he was in his twenties. He had a small scar on his forehead.

It was in the same spot that Naomi was currently holding his hand to.

Wait. Is he... Oh God. He has to be...

"I'm you, Katagaki Naomi. From ten years in the future."

"You're...what?" Naomi repeated numbly. "The future...?"

He fully understood, at last, what was going on.

Strangely, this made perfect sense to him. It filled in all the blanks and lined up perfectly with the events of these last two days. It all fit together.

There was just one problem.

Was something so absurd *really* possible?

In a science fiction novel, sure. In a movie, absolutely. It was the sort of story you saw all the time in comics and video games. But it wasn't something that happened in real life.

But then again...this man was telling him that this world *wasn't* real. He was claiming Naomi lived in a simulation of the past, and that he'd somehow broken into it from the future.

"Don't be scared."

Startled, Naomi looked up again. The man was staring down at him with a little smile on his face. His voice sounded almost gentle, in a way it never had before.

"Rest assured, you've got nothing to worry about. I know all about you. You're *me*, after all." The man's voice was soothing and kind. Striding up to Naomi, he bent down on one knee to bring their faces closer together.

I have to say something, Naomi thought. But his bewilderment wasn't going away. Finding the right words felt impossible.

"Don't say anything," the man said gently. "I understand."

In that moment, Naomi felt *reassured* in a strange way he'd never experienced before. It felt a bit like...he was with an old friend who knew him intimately. Or a family member who he completely trusted.

This man *was* Naomi. He knew *everything* about him.

In that case, he had to know what Naomi was going through right now.

He knew about his frustration, his anguish, and his failed attempts to change.

"That's right. That's the reason I came here," Naomi's other self murmured quietly. "I know what you're thinking..."

Naomi's heart thudded loudly in his chest. He stared up at the older man with the expression of a trusting little brother.

The man continued, his eyes full of compassion.

"You want a *girlfriend*."

"Uh, not really..."

The Takano River gurgled softly along, oblivious to the awkward silence between them.

CHAPTER TWO

1.

NAOMI TENTATIVELY touched the large, square bandage on his forehead.

"I can't believe *you* got yourself hurt, Naomi," said his mother, sounding genuinely mystified by this turn of events. Naomi had always spent most of his time safely indoors. He'd gotten through elementary and middle school without a single major injury to speak of.

Grimacing awkwardly, Naomi gave the bandage another careful rub. There was no telling how many years this thing had been sitting in their closet.

"I did give the city government a call about that drone, for what it's worth..."

"Don't worry about it, Mom," said Naomi hurriedly. "It's just a scratch. Thanks."

Increasingly embarrassed by the entire situation, he quickly left the living room and opened the sliding door to his bedroom, which was located two paces down the hall.

Unsurprisingly, his new *friend* was waiting for him in there. He hadn't expected anything else, but it was still unsettling.

Naomi slid the door shut behind him and sized up the man warily.

He was still wearing his pure white coat, even inside the house. He'd kept his hood down, though, so his face was now clearly visible. That three-legged bird, which seemed to be his companion, was perched on his shoulder.

This man had just claimed to *be* Naomi. Or a version of him from the future, anyway. At the moment, he was studying Naomi's bookshelves.

Naomi took the opportunity to study his face from the side. There was a resemblance there, to be sure. Ten years from now, he might look something like this.

At the same time, he didn't *want* to believe that it was true. It was hard to express why, but...he didn't *like* adults like this guy. The man was always giving orders and bossing him around. He didn't pay any attention to Naomi's feelings and constantly ignored his questions. All he cared about was getting what he wanted.

His personality felt like the polar opposite of Naomi's. It was really hard to believe he'd turn into someone like this.

"Ha, I remember buying this."

Naomi started. The man was pointing at the book that lay open on his desk. It was the one he'd bought two days ago and had already filled with colorful sticky notes: *How to Be Decisive: A Better You by Tomorrow!*

There was a small smile on the man's face, practically a self-mocking smirk.

Naomi approached the man cautiously. There was a significant height difference between them; in close quarters, he was forced to look up at him.

After a moment, he managed to piece together enough words to form a question. "Are you *really* me?"

"What, you wondering about my height?"

Naomi nodded nervously. That was exactly what he'd been wondering about. He wasn't even 170 centimeters tall, but this man was well over 180.

"You'll keep growing for a while," the man replied simply. "That said, this is a just an avatar. I could change its appearance any way I wanted to."

"What? Like how?"

The man lightly snapped his fingers. His hand instantly disappeared, replaced by a shiny, metallic arm.

Naomi stared at it, wide-eyed with shock. It was like a magic trick. The man's hand had turned into a simple two-pronged claw, reminiscent of a toy you might see gathering dust on the shelves of a pawn shop. It clacked open and shut a few times, then abruptly returned to its original form.

"Huh," Naomi said, for lack of any better thoughts. That transformation had been far too quick and realistic to be a sleight-of-hand trick. He couldn't even imagine how that would work.

This was just...overwhelming. Naomi dropped down heavily

onto his chair. He studied his own hands, trying to make sense of things.

Thinking back to what they'd talked about earlier, he lifted his right hand and snapped his fingers. They produced a sound, if not a particularly impressive one. Naturally, nothing else happened.

Still, he could *feel* his hand. He could feel his fingers. They sure as hell felt real to him.

"So this whole world, uh..." Naomi said, turning his head up to look at the man. "It's really just made up of data? It's some kind of simulation?"

"Yeah. Not that it really matters much. This world is a complete, *perfect* copy of reality, preserved inside the AllTale system."

Once again, without prelude, the man snapped his fingers. Naomi jumped a little. But nothing changed this time.

"Now I'm back in reality."

Again, the man snapped his fingers. Again, nothing happened.

"And now I'm in the simulation. I can hop freely between the two. But since this world is *your* reality, you can't tell it's simulated. You'll never be able to perceive it as anything but real, so it's pointless to even try."

"Well, okay. I guess I'll have to take your word for it."

"Huh. You sure took that well."

"The whole thing kind of reminds me of Egan, I guess..." Naomi glanced at the small shelf next to his desk, where he kept books he was particularly fond of. Quite a few of these were "blue-back" science fiction paperbacks from Hayakawa

Publishing. Writers like Greg Egan, H. G. Wells, Phillip K. Dick, and Arthur C. Clarke were all well represented. He was really fond of their work.

Naomi hadn't intended to build an SF-heavy collection, but at some point he'd fallen in love with the genre. In the very beginning, he'd been a bit intimidated by the ominous-looking covers and the thickness of the novels, but now he actively looked for books like that every time he visited the store.

He'd read quite a lot of science fiction for a boy his age. In a way, he'd given himself a good foundation for coping with this hooded man's strange claims.

As his eyes ran across the spines of the books on his shelf, Naomi thought back to the stories they contained. *Permutation City* by Greg Egan had a setup a lot like what this man was describing. And *Incandescence*, too.

Those books had both featured purely simulated worlds. The people living in them were simulations, too. Thinking about those stories helped him process the situation, at least a little bit. But it also led him to new questions.

Incandescence was a story set in the distant future, when almost all of humanity had been converted into digital transhumans. And in *Permutation City*, the simulated world was very different from reality.

But according to the hooded man, this simulation was a "record"—an exact copy of the real world as it used to be.

"If that's all true," said Naomi, looking up again, "why are you here? Why come visit a copy of the past?"

It was the first question that had popped into his mind. What was his future self even *doing* here?

"I think I already gave you an answer, but I don't mind repeating myself."

The man snapped his fingers again. This time, there was a visible effect. The bird leapt off his shoulder, flapping up to the top of a bookshelf.

With skillful movement of its three legs, it kicked down the cardboard box that was sitting there.

"Gah!"

The box hit the ground with a thump and fell over, spilling its contents onto the ground.

Naomi had packed it and put it up there—it was full of magazines. *Gravure* magazines, mostly. And a few that were slightly more explicit.

"Ah! Gaaaah!"

Yelping with embarrassment, Naomi dove onto the pile. Gathering the magazines in his arms, he pushed them under his bed. It was far too late, of course, but he couldn't stop himself.

He could feel his face going red. Wasn't this man his future self? Shouldn't he be humiliated by this, too?

"I came here to help you with the painful dilemmas of your youth," the man said, his voice as bold as ever. "In other words, I'm here to help you get a girlfriend."

2.

EVERY CLASS in a school is surrounded by a strange barrier. Anyone can enter or leave their own classroom freely. However, if you want to enter a *different* class, you've got to contend with an invisible wall. You might just be going to see a friend across the hall, but the moment you cross that threshold, the other thirty-nine students in the room will suddenly seem like enemies determined to drive you from their turf.

Because of this, Naomi *never* set foot in other classes. Even a handful of people glancing in his direction was more than he could bear. The very thought of an entire classroom looking at him made him want to run screaming for the hills.

It was kind of pathetic, yes. He was probably the single weakest, most fragile person out of all two hundred fifty first-year students in his school.

But there were also people on the opposite end of the spectrum: unusually *powerful* exceptions. The ones who had both self-confidence and respect from others, for example. Or people who could find their own way through anything that life threw at them.

While pretending to read a paperback at his desk, Naomi glanced repeatedly across the room. He was so worried about not being noticed that he could only manage to look for about two seconds at a time. But he couldn't bring himself to stop, either.

Three girls were chatting at the center of the classroom. Two of them were from Naomi's class, but the girl sitting in between them was from the next room over. She was constantly smiling or bursting into laughter, and the air around her seemed to fill with sparkles whenever it happened.

She was Kadenokouji Misuzu, the "idol" Naomi had first spotted at the library committee. Over the course of that single meeting, she'd somehow captured the hearts of multiple boys her own age, along with several older guys. She was a force to be reckoned with. It was hard to believe she was the same age as Naomi.

Of course, the girl herself probably didn't have any interest in the school's hierarchy as Naomi saw it. She probably didn't even know it existed. That was part of what made her so fearsome.

It didn't matter whether a real princess was strong or fragile—her presence was all that was required. Just by being in the room, she made everyone else in it happy. Anyone standing in her way would smile and yield the path to her. She could walk right into any classroom she wanted without a second thought. Everyone was actually *happy* to see her!

Hidden behind his paperback, Naomi continued to observe this strange phenomenon. Misuzu was smiling again, her face emitting magical beams of sunshine in all directions.

Man, thought Naomi. *I kind of wish I was observing her instead...*

"Kadenon! Let's get back to our classroom!" another girl called from the doorway. Misuzu nodded and rose to her feet.

"Gotta go! See you at lunch, okay?"

With a little wave to her friends, she left the classroom at a trot. Once she was gone, Naomi could finally see all the way over to the other side of the room.

In one of the seats next to the window, a girl was quietly reading a book. There was a cover on it, but it looked like a novel.

She was doing the exact same thing as Naomi, in other words. But Naomi didn't feel the comparison was fair to her. She was reading in a fundamentally different way.

"Pass! Pass!"

A sudden shout made Naomi flinch. A group of boys were tossing a bag of gym clothes around the room as a makeshift basketball.

"Come on, cut it ooout!" someone shouted, their tone only half serious.

Naomi looked back down at his book, wishing he could hide behind it. Those guys were the same age as him. So why did they seem so *intimidating?*

"Hey!"

"Crap!"

Naomi looked up. Somebody had messed up and sent the bag flying off course. It zipped across the room, passing *between* the girl at the window and her book; it hit the glass loudly and fell to the floor.

The classroom was suddenly dead silent. Everyone was thinking the same thing: *This isn't good.*

The bag hadn't hit her, but it easily could have. The boys had clearly gone too far. Everyone, including Naomi, waited anxiously for the girl's reaction.

Flip.

She'd turned to the next page in her book.

Everyone else in the room blinked simultaneously. Nobody actually spoke, but the word "*whoa*" was definitely running through their minds.

The culprit who'd hurled the bag received a sharp elbow to the side and promptly ducked his head in apology. "Sorry 'bout that..."

Ichigyou Ruri kept right on reading her book as if nothing had happened.

After observing her for an entire day, Naomi discovered that his fellow library committee member, Ichigyou Ruri, was a very *formidable* person in many ways.

First of all, her face was formidable.

That word could mean more than one thing, of course. Some people might be described as *formidably beautiful.* But Naomi wasn't entirely sure whether that applied in this case. He thought she had a pretty face, but not one that stood out to him as his type. She certainly couldn't be called *cute.*

Ruri had a very composed face. She didn't smile, and her default expression was cold and calm—almost angry, really. Most of the people in their grade would laugh at pretty much anything, even if it wasn't funny, but Ruri's face suggested that she didn't do much laughing at all. She looked like the kind of person who would sit stone-faced through an entire comedy routine out of pure stubbornness.

At lunchtime, Ruri headed to the school store.

She was relatively tall compared to someone like Kadenokouji Misuzu, granted, but Naomi had still been impressed to see her push right through the crowd without flinching or hesitating. Reaching the front of the pack while plenty of fish sandwiches and yakisoba breads were still available, she'd immediately called out, "I'd like four twisty breads, please."

Apparently, she was a fan of those things.

After buying her lunch and returning to the classroom, Ruri found her seat occupied by a girl who was chattering cheerfully with a group of friends.

"So yeah, you know what Yukawa-senpai told me next? Seriously, he—"

"That's my seat," Ruri interrupted.

Naomi cringed a little. Her timing was *terrible*. It was like she wasn't even trying to be nice.

The group of girls apologized and moved across the classroom. Ichigyou Ruri, looking totally unperturbed, promptly sat down and resumed her reading while working on her twisty breads.

After school, Ruri was on duty at the checkout desk of the library. The majority of the job was loaning out books and processing returns, but there usually weren't that many people using the library on any given day, so they usually had lots of free time on their hands.

Unsurprisingly, she used that time to read her book.

After engrossing herself in it for a while, a sudden frown

appeared on Ruri's face. Her default expression was already vaguely hostile, but now she was *clearly* displeased. Naomi was reminded of a scowling juvenile delinquent from a manga he'd once read.

Ruri began flipping backward through her book. After finding something or other in the first few pages, she returned to the page she'd been reading and grimaced once again. She didn't even notice that someone was now standing by the desk, hoping to borrow a book. And the poor guy was too intimidated to speak up.

Naomi, who'd been watching from the hallway, quietly expressed his thoughts—which were probably shared by anyone else who'd witnessed this.

"Yikes..."

At that point, something smacked into the back of his head. Turning around, he found the three-legged bird flapping in the air behind him.

"Kaw!"

With that brief cry, the bird flapped down to land on the hallway floor. Then, it turned around and walked off at a steady trot. Naomi tagged along behind it.

As he followed the chubby little animal, Naomi studied it curiously from behind. From what he'd found on the internet, a bird like this was apparently called a *yatagarasu*. He felt like he'd seen a depiction of one on an informational sign at some shrine before, although he couldn't remember which. In any case, it was supposedly a very special kind of crow.

The crow trotted along the hallway at a surprisingly brisk clip, perhaps aided by its extra leg. Naomi jogged behind it at first, but eventually he had to run just to keep up.

Finally, the crow turned into a boy's bathroom on the very edge of the building, one that didn't get much traffic. Following it inside, Naomi found his "future self" waiting with his arms folded.

"Why are we meeting—"

"Shh," the man interrupted him, holding up a hand. A moment later, there was the sound of a toilet flushing, and an older student emerged from one of the stalls. As he washed his hands, he glanced dubiously over at Naomi, who was just standing there awkwardly.

Once the other student had left the bathroom, the older man lowered his hand, signaling that it was all right to proceed.

"You can't just start *talking to yourself* when other people are around, you know. People might think you're nuts."

"Thanks. Very considerate of you..."

For what little it was worth, this future version of Naomi did have *some* consideration for his reputation. Naomi was grateful for that, but not *too* grateful. He wouldn't even have this problem if the man had never come here, after all.

"So, did you get a good look at her today?"

"Uh, yeah."

Naomi had carried out his mission exactly as instructed. He'd observed his target carefully for the entire day.

"I kept an eye on her all day, but... Uhm, are you *sure* it's her?"

"I am," the man said. "You and Ichigyou Ruri will be dating three months from today." The way he said it made it sound like the most obvious statement in the world.

Naomi frowned involuntarily. His feelings about all this were very mixed.

"What's with that face, huh?"

"Um, well…I don't know." Naomi waved a hand in a vague gesture of protest. "Me and Ichigyou-san? It seems kind of… impossible."

"Impossible? Why?"

"Well, I mean…" Naomi paused, trying to find the right words. He was a little frightened of the man, so he wanted to explain this as diplomatically as possible. "I'm not sure I could handle her. She's kind of a lone wolf, and I'm more of a wimp. I feel like she'll bite me if I get too close. Also, um, I kind of prefer girls on the cuter side of the spectrum, so…"

"What? Are you calling her *ugly*?"

Apparently, Naomi had blundered straight into a landmine. He suppressed an urge to cover his face with his hands.

In his mind's eye, he pictured Ichigyou Ruri as accurately as he could.

I mean… Come on…

"Of course not! I think she's got a really pretty face. But she's just not the *cute* type, right?!"

Naomi tried his very best to explain his position; he was scared, but he wasn't going to lie to himself. If the cold, fearsome face of Ichigyou Ruri was *cute,* then so was a snarling lion.

"Wrong!" shouted the man angrily. "She's the cutest girl on the planet Earth. Are you blind or something, kid? Are you sure you were even watching the right person?!"

That was actually seeming kind of plausible to Naomi right now. Maybe there had been a mistake. Maybe he was actually going to be dating some *other* girl in three months' time.

Still...you could misremember someone's face, but the man knew her name perfectly...

As Naomi pondered this mystery, the older man suddenly strode toward him and passed right through his body. "I'll just have to double-check myself."

"Huh?"

"She's in the library, right? Follow me, but *don't* say anything!"

With that final declaration, the man passed right through the bathroom door. In his hurry to follow, Naomi nearly walked right into it.

3.

THE OLDER MAN STRODE right into the library as if its glass door didn't even exist.

Naomi screeched to a halt in front of it, then slowly opened the heavy door. When he entered the room, he found himself in a hushed, peaceful space. He walked cautiously into this holy ground, conscious that it was taboo to make a sound here.

Nishiki High's main building had undergone a major remodel

a few years earlier, and its library had been completely redesigned in a very modern style. The interior was a pleasant mix of clean white and polished wood.

The library was two floors with an atrium in its center. The first floor was home to the book collection, and the second floor was a study space. Since the students who came here to study were up on the second floor, the browsing space on the first floor was usually open. There weren't many people hanging around today, either.

Naomi moved from one bookshelf to the other, trying to be stealthy. This place ought to be his home turf, but he felt more like a burglar sneaking into someone else's home.

The older man had stopped next to a shelf not far from the checkout desk and was gazing quietly at it. Naomi crouched down next to him and pointed at Ruri. "See?" he whispered. "That's Ichigyou-san right there."

Ruri was still reading at the checkout desk. It was probably the same book she'd been working on earlier, judging from the displeased expression on her face.

"I mean, she's the only other library committee member from my class, so I don't think you could have mixed things up, but..."

As he said it, Naomi realized the idea really didn't make much sense. This girl was the only Ichigyou Ruri he knew; he couldn't imagine that some other person with the same name was going to show up and become his girlfriend out of nowhere.

Still, the other scenario seemed equally implausible. He couldn't even imagine how he would start dating *this* girl in only three months. They'd happened to become classmates in high school and happened to end up on the same committee, but that was as far as their connection went.

Sure, those coincidences might be enough to lead to a friendship at some point. Maybe. Possibly. But at the moment, their ties were totally superficial. And this girl was so *different* from Naomi.

Her personality was nothing like his. She was so much stronger than him. It felt like they were different *kinds* of people on some fundamental level. A giant, yawning chasm separated the two of them, and Naomi had no idea how he could ever hope to cross it.

He couldn't really imagine himself falling in love with her. But just as he thought that, a drop of something fell past his eyes. Naomi looked up.

There were tears running down the invisible man's cheeks.

Naomi found himself at a loss for words. This felt like seeing something that he shouldn't. And yet, he couldn't look away.

The man stared fixedly at the counter with wide eyes. His tears flowed freely, but he didn't even wipe them away. He just gazed at the girl behind the desk and, for a long, awkward moment, everyone in the room seemed frozen in place.

The tears of Naomi's "future self" passed right through the floor of the library and disappeared.

4.

THE STREETS OF KYOTO were bathed in orange light.

Naomi looked down on them from the rooftop of his school building. The man that only he could see was standing on top of the low guard wall at its very edge. He probably wasn't in any danger, but it made Naomi nervous anyway.

Naturally, Naomi wasn't up there with him. He was leaning against the wall with his feet safely on the roof.

From up here, he had a clear view of the big apartment buildings around Shijo-Omiya, and the mountains further out. Kyoto was surrounded by mountains on all sides, so you could see them any way you looked, and soon, the sun would sink below them.

"The accident took place not long after we started dating," the man said quietly.

Naomi looked up at him curiously. He'd put up his hood again, so it was impossible to see his expression.

"The two of us went to see the fireworks together. It was a cloudy day, so they'd considered canceling the show, but they decided to rush through it before the rain started. And then, just as the show reached its climax, a bolt of lightning hit a tree on the riverbank."

Naomi's heart thudded in his chest, and a cold shiver ran down his spine. Somehow, his body knew what was coming next.

"Unfortunately, Ruri was standing right next to it..." The man paused, then continued solemnly, "and she never opened her eyes again."

He fell silent. The sounds of cars in the distance seemed oddly loud all of a sudden. Naomi needed some time to process what he'd just heard. This was far more serious than he'd expected.

This man was telling him that Ichigyou Ruri had died.

Honestly, it wasn't easy to believe. He'd only met the girl recently, and he'd seen her alive and well only minutes earlier. But this man was talking about the future, so of course it didn't feel real—her death hadn't happened yet.

There was one thing Naomi *could* believe, though...because he'd seen it with his own two eyes. This arrogant, self-confident man who claimed to be his future self had broken down in tears.

"My objective is to *falsify* the record of that event," the man continued. "We'll prevent the accident three months from now, overwriting it completely. When she survives, it should create a ripple effect through the simulation as a whole. Within AllTale's infinite storage space, a world where Ichigyou Ruri survived will form."

Naomi thought this through as best he could. The man's words fit with what he knew, at least. If this AllTale system really did have *infinite* capacity, creating a new world might be possible.

He had one question, though.

"Uh..." Naomi started to speak, but his voice faltered for a moment. "Is there...any point to doing that?"

The words came out sounding hesitant and fearful. Naomi found himself looking down at his shoes. Maybe he shouldn't have asked, but he hadn't been able to resist the urge.

"Even if you save Ichigyou-san inside the simulation..."

"She won't come back in the real world," the man responded in a perfectly matter-of-fact tone.

"Then why do it?"

There was a lengthy silence. After a while, the man's mouth quirked into a smile.

"You know, it happened *just* after we started going out." He reached up and pulled down his hood before continuing, exposing his face again. "We never got a chance to go anywhere together. We didn't make any memories. We didn't even take a single picture together." There was no intensity or anger to the way he spoke.

"I just want one smile." He continued, quietly and earnestly. "Just once, I want to see her really, truly happy. I want a record of that to exist. I want that memory. Even if it's not real."

The man's gaze turned to Naomi.

"Even if she's not smiling at *me*."

Naomi could see the determination in his eyes. It was deep, and strong, and completely beyond his understanding.

Maybe it was meaningless. Maybe this was all a simulation. Maybe the girl he'd loved would really be dating "someone else." But this man was still going to make it happen.

Hopping down from the wall, the man approached Naomi, who found himself frozen. He tensed up reflexively as the man reached for his arm, but the hand didn't make contact. It just passed right through him.

"I can't do much here. This is only an avatar, unable to touch anything in this world. I'm powerless on my own."

With that, he took one step back and bowed his head deeply.

"Please help me, Naomi."

His words were simple and straightforward. Maybe that was why they hit Naomi as hard as they did.

Naomi was at a total loss for words; this imposing, intimidating man, this confident and arrogant adult, was *bowing* to him. *Begging* him for help.

"Look, uh..."

Naomi's hands rose up defensively. He hadn't yet decided how to respond, but his body seemed ready to reject this plea.

His mind, on the other hand, wanted time to think this through. This man was asking him earnestly for help. He'd been honest with Naomi and told him the whole story. Naomi owed him a thoughtful response.

"Okay, well..." With a conscious effort, Naomi lowered his hands. "This is all new to me, and it hasn't really sunk in yet. I don't know Ichigyou-san that well, either. So, um, I can't really imagine going out with her, but..."

He mentally ran through the words he'd just spoken. He still couldn't imagine dating her, at all.

But that said—

"I mean, maybe she's not the *cute* type, exactly, but...uh, it *would* be nice to have a girlfriend that pretty..." Naomi's halting, stumbling words came out sounding painfully crass and selfish, but there wasn't much he could do about that. He was only being honest.

"Also..." The words flowed more easily now. "If we *can* stop that accident from happening, and save her life...I want to do it. I *want* to save her."

Naomi's future self looked up with an expression of surprise.

"Um..."

Naomi forced a dopey smile on his face in an attempt to disguise his embarrassment. It felt a bit pathetic, even to him.

"So what am I supposed to call you, anyway? I mean, you're me."

The man smiled. That familiar confidence was returning to his face, and for some reason, that made Naomi happy.

"You can call me Sensei," he said, finally straightening up out of his bow.

"Sensei? Like you're my mentor or something? I mean, I guess that works..." It was funny—the kanji that make up the word Sensei mean "previous," and "life." Naomi wondered if that was intentional.

He was also kind of impressed—it took guts to give yourself a nickname like that. It wasn't the choice *he* would have made. Apparently he was going to acquire a lot more self-confidence at some point in the next ten years.

Sensei reached out his right hand.

Naomi stared at it uncertainly. The two of them couldn't touch each other.

"It's just a ritual. Can't hurt to go through the motions," Sensei said.

Naomi nodded and reached out as well. Their hands clasped awkwardly in midair, both gripping at something that wasn't there.

They didn't make physical contact in that moment, but they *did* make a pact. Naomi was going to help Sensei, and together, they would save Ichigyou Ruri's life.

"I'll teach you all sorts of things. I do have ten years more experience than you, after all."

"So how can I help?" He was finally feeling calmer, so he could consider the details of this arrangement better than before.

Sensei claimed he couldn't touch this world directly. In that case, Naomi would probably be at least somewhat useful, since he could interact with it freely. That said, he was only a high-school student, and not a particularly competent one. He was a weak-willed waffler who couldn't even make his own decisions.

"I can't do anything special. I'm kind of useless, really. I'm sure you know that..." He hadn't intended to put himself down, but this was the truth—there was no point running from it.

Sensei answered him with a bold smile.

"Wrong. You can do *anything*."

Suddenly, a black shadow jumped across the roof. Naomi jerked his head up to look for its source. That three-legged crow had taken flight again.

"Right now, you've got me on your side..."

It was flying right at them. Specifically right at their hands, still "shaking" in midair. Naomi couldn't jerk away in time.

The bird flew into his hand—and quickly began to transform.

"And you've got this guy, too."

The thing that had been a crow distorted itself into a soft, supple substance, wrapping itself around Naomi's hand. It spread over his palm, between his fingers, then down to his wrist; the sensation was like nothing he'd ever felt before.

For just an instant, he though he saw a spray of feathers in the air. When the dust had settled, Naomi looked down at his right hand. It was covered in an odd blue glove with a surface that swayed like the waters of a deep and ancient sea.

CHAPTER THREE

1.

NAOMI STUFFED HIS BACKPACK with textbooks and a school uniform.

He was wearing a sweatsuit today. It wasn't his typical outfit, so putting it on felt a bit exciting, almost like he was on his way to a class trip or something.

Leaving his bedroom, he slid the door shut quietly behind him, then snuck down the hallway toward the front door. As he started to turn its doorknob, he heard his mother stirring in her room.

"Naomi?" she called sleepily.

Naomi had thought up an excuse for his early-morning outing, but if he could leave without being forced to explain, that was definitely better.

"I'll see you later!"

Hurriedly stepping outside, he closed and locked the door behind him, then rushed down the apartment building stairs. Making a beeline for the first-floor storage area, he grabbed his bike and hopped on.

Once he got moving, he realized it was chillier out than he'd expected. Although it was April now, it was still brisk outside at 6 a.m. Maybe he should have brought a jacket or something.

Naomi made his way across Nishioji Street, savoring its unusual emptiness.

His destination today was Narabigaoka, a well-known scenic spot a few blocks from Hanazono Station. It was a gently sloping hill, its surface lushly green and dotted with ancient tombs; it rose to a height of roughly fifty meters above the residential neighborhood that had grown up around it. It reminded Naomi of the hill behind the school in *Doraemon*.

There were maintained walking paths running through the mountain itself, popular with hikers seeking a little light exertion. Today, though, Naomi had ventured off the beaten path and wandered deep into the trees.

Eventually, he found himself standing with Sensei in a small clearing surrounded by dense foliage—a secluded corner of the forest, a place where no one ever went.

"Start by picturing the *result* you want." Sensei was giving Naomi a lesson—living up to his name, he approached it almost like a lecture. "Make your mental image as vivid as possible. Start with something very familiar and very simple. Plastic, rubber, paper, whatever."

Naomi closed his eyes and focused.

He was kneeling in the dirt with his right hand pressed against the ground. On that hand, he wore the glove that the odd crow had turned itself into.

Now that his eyes were shut, the image in his mind seemed to grow just a little clearer. At first he'd tried to imagine a sheet of paper, but that just made the image of a novel pop into his mind; he'd ended up switching to plastic instead.

He visualized a small plastic block—a plain, unremarkable lump of raw material.

Gradually, he felt the sensation of the dirt beneath his hand begin to change. It wasn't a sudden, dramatic change; it felt like the area was being slowly drained of both warmth and coldness, somehow growing less *defined*. It wasn't something he'd ever felt before.

"Now reach out your hand in your mind's eye, and..." Sensei paused, as if waiting for the right moment.

"Grab it!"

At that forceful command, Naomi visualized his hand grasping the piece of plastic. His *actual* right hand moved as well, grabbing reflexively at the ground, and somehow, it actually took hold of something.

His hand, which had been pressed firmly against the dirt, reached down *into* it. It felt like the hard-packed earth had suddenly grown soft and pliable, allowing his fingers to sink right through it.

Startled, Naomi's eyes snapped open.

His hand was still touching the ground, its fingers spread wide. Had that sensation been an illusion, then? It had felt so *real*. He lifted his hand off the ground and revealed a small object. A white lump of plastic in the shape of a hexagon.

It was exactly what he'd visualized.

"It worked! It actually worked!" Naomi cried. Snatching up the object, he poked at it gingerly with his naked left hand. It looked and felt exactly like a normal piece of plastic.

"Not bad for your first try," said Sensei with a tone of mild satisfaction. He drew a little closer and pointed at the strange glove on Naomi's hand. "That's the God Hand."

As he spoke, Sensei snapped his fingers.

In an instant, a glove appeared on his right hand, the exact same one that Naomi was currently wearing. This startled him for a moment, but then he realized it likely wasn't real. Sensei had transformed his arm into that goofy metal claw the other day, after all—this was probably more of the same, just a copy of the glove on his avatar.

Sensei turned his hand so the palm faced upward.

"The God Hand works by directly accessing the data All-Tale uses to generate this simulation. It can rewrite the fabric of this world."

Suddenly, water started pouring out of Sensei's hand. The flow grew faster and faster until it was gushing out in torrents.

"You can turn air into water."

The water stopped coming, then disappeared entirely. Sensei squatted down and put his hand to the ground. When he opened it again, an enormous gem the size of Naomi's fist had appeared inside it.

"Dirt into precious stones."

With a wave of his hand, the gem disappeared too. Sensei got back to his feet. This time, he grabbed at the empty air.

His hand seemed to close around an invisible cylinder. In answer to the motion, a solid substance took shape in midair. A white metal rod grew down to the ground; after a moment, Naomi realized it was the pole of a traffic sign.

"Nothing into something."

Sensei grabbed the sign he'd just created. The thing was solid metal and more than two meters in length, but he swung it around like a baton. In the blink of an eye, it had also disappeared.

"All that was just an illusion," he continued. "I'm only an avatar, so my access rights within AllTale are strictly limited. I can't interact with anything in this world, so showing you some magic tricks is the best I can do."

Sensei's eyes turned down to his illusionary glove.

"But the God Hand has the permissions necessary to change this world on a physical level. It can touch objects in this world and interfere with their reality. Once you learn how to use that thing, you'll be able to do all the tricks I just showed you for real."

Once again, Naomi looked at his hand. Did that mean—

"So, I can do *anything*, basically?"

"In theory, sure. But there are a number of important limitations." Once again, Sensei squatted down.

"First of all," he said as he touched the ground with his glove and pulled up a free-standing whiteboard out of the dirt, "the glove can only rewrite things it's in direct physical contact with."

He turned the palm of his hand toward Naomi. Naomi

flinched, expecting something to pop out at him, but nothing happened.

"You can't use the glove to create something at a distance."

"O-okay..."

"Secondly..." Sensei snapped his fingers, and illustrations and writing appeared in marker across the surface of the whiteboard. Naomi hurried over and sat down on his knees in front of it. "The time it takes to execute your commands will depend on the amount of data being altered."

Naomi stared up at the board. There were chemical symbols and molecular diagrams sketched out on its surface: Fe, Cu, O_2, H_2O. All very simple molecules even he could make sense of.

"When we're dealing with simple substances—stuff like water that has a very basic structure—it's all quite simple. You can make that sort of thing easily and delete it just as fast."

Naomi nodded. That was an easy enough concept to grasp.

"When it comes to complex objects, though, any modification will take time, and you may struggle to visualize them in sufficient detail. Intricate devices like PCs or smartphones are particularly tough. Same goes for manufactured machinery with a million different parts."

Naomi considered the point. He might be able to create a passable imitation of the *exterior* of a car if pressed, but he had no idea what the interior components looked like. The same applied to computers.

"And of course, the most difficult of all to modify are living things."

Sensei snapped his fingers. The writing on the whiteboard instantly changed, and new drawings appeared there, simple sketches of a dog, a cat, and a human being.

"Does that apply to *everything* that's alive?"

"All living things are in a constant state of change. They require a vast amount of data to simulate. Here's a quick question, on that note..." Sensei pointed a finger at Naomi. "Name the part of the human body that contains the largest quantity of data."

"Um—" All the body parts and organs Naomi knew spun through his head, but after a moment, the wheel stopped at the most obvious answer.

"The brain?"

Sensei nodded, and Naomi breathed a quiet sigh of relief.

"The human brain's storage capacity is enormous, and its contents are constantly shifting over time. Human consciousness, the manifestation of those contents, is essentially the densest possible form of information. Even with the God Hand, messing with that would be difficult."

Naomi studied the thing he was wearing on his hand once again.

When Sensei had first described it, he'd assumed it was an all-powerful tool. Something capable of rewriting *the fabric of reality* should be able to change literally anything in this world. A part of him had hoped it might make impossible-seeming things very easy—like going out with Ichigyou Ruri.

The very idea still struck him as ridiculous, honestly. Naomi knew he wasn't particularly appealing, even compared to other guys his age. He couldn't think of a single reason why she would ever be attracted to him. They were supposedly going to start going out at some point in the future, but that seemed like an embarrassing fantasy right now.

And yet, this glove could rewrite the world. He'd hoped it could just...resolve the whole thing instantly, somehow.

Sensei had already snuffed out that brief glimmer of hope. The God Hand couldn't make her fall in love with him, even if he wanted it to.

"I made that thing to help you prevent the accident." When Naomi looked up, he found that Sensei was shaking his head in disapproval. "It's not going to help you on the romantic front."

There he goes reading my mind again...

Naomi averted his eyes awkwardly. Sensei *was* him, in a sense, so of course he'd know what he was thinking. That also made it impossible to deflect the criticism. All he could really do was pout.

What am I supposed to do, then? he thought, staring resentfully at the older man. *If you know everything about me, you know I'm not capable of flirting with a girl.*

Looking like he'd received that telepathic message, Sensei smirked evilly.

"Weren't you listening to me last time? You can do *anything* now, Naomi." He reached inside his coat. "The God Hand's job is to prevent the accident..."

When he pulled his hand out, it was holding a notebook. It was a perfectly ordinary thing with a blue cover and a brand logo on the front, the kind used by college students. But judging from its tattered condition, it had been in active use for quite some time.

"And it's *my* job to help you get the girl."

On the cover of that notebook were the words: *Ultimate Manual.*

2.

IN KYOTO, THE BUSES were *always* crowded. You started off with that as a baseline, and then guessed *how* crowded it would be based on the route and the time of day.

For example, the morning rush hour in spring would see commuters jostling alongside tourists and kids on school trips. The buses got so overstuffed that no one could get on them for hours at a time. Once things got that bad, it was usually best to give up and tell yourself they weren't running at all.

Comparatively speaking, the bus Naomi was currently riding wasn't too packed. He was on the 13 Line a bit after 3 p.m, well before the evening rush, but after the flow of tourists had slowed down. Even so, the seats were all taken by sightseers heading to

Nijo Castle or Kinkaku Temple. Six people, including Naomi, stood in the aisles.

Holding a strap with one hand, Naomi kept his phone up to his mouth with the other. A cord snaked from it to the earphones he was wearing. To anyone who saw him, it would look like he was on a phone call.

Naomi glanced to his side. Sensei was standing there, holding his tattered notebook open in his hands.

"On April 20th," he read out in a voice only Naomi could hear, "I took the bus to borrow a book from the Kita branch of the city library."

Naomi leaned over to look at the notebook and Sensei obligingly turned it in his direction. Thanks to their height difference, it was right at eye level. The pages were covered in text. There were numerous dated entries, each accompanied by handwritten descriptions of various mundane events.

"Something happened that day to bring the two of us a bit closer together," Sensei said.

Naomi brought his phone a little closer to his mouth. This was a technique he'd thought up after humiliating himself the other day—a way to talk with Sensei in public without attracting attention. He'd just pretend he was on the phone with someone, instead of speaking to an invisible person standing next to him. It wasn't especially polite behavior, but it beat getting looked at like some kind of lunatic.

"So, in other words," he said, his voice soft with anxiety, "I just have to do what you did back then, Sensei. And then I'll end up dating her, just like in the history AllTale recorded."

He was thinking it over even as he spoke the words. It did seem obvious enough, really. If Sensei was telling the truth about the way things had turned out with Ruri, then events would naturally proceed in that direction.

But in that case—

"Couldn't you just do nothing at all, then? Maybe we should just let things take their normal course."

It couldn't hurt to throw the idea out there. If events were going to move forward on their own, their efforts might backfire.

"Remember what I told you on the roof, Naomi," Sensei replied sharply. "AllTale has infinite storage capacity. When one section of its records changes, it generates a whole string of brand-new events."

Naomi nodded. That was the only reason Sensei's plan to save Ruri's life was even possible.

"The same thing's happening right now, even as we speak. When I came here from the future, my presence immediately began to alter the course this world was taking."

"Oh. Then things started changing the moment we met?"

"That's right. The divergence was small at first, but over time, it's going to grow more pronounced. There's no telling how far off track things might get if we sit on our hands. That's why you need to make an active effort to stay on the rails."

"Hmm, I see..."

Naomi nodded knowingly, but in all honesty, he didn't *really* get it. Sensei was his only source of information on how all this worked, though. He had to take his word for it on this stuff.

As Sensei had repeatedly pointed out, Naomi was a resident of this world. The system that kept it running was beyond his comprehension. It didn't matter what was happening to the data behind the scenes—he could only perceive his own life as a single chain of *events*.

Naomi found himself looking up at Sensei's face. This man had broken free of that chain. He'd chosen to step back in time and participate in a retake version of his own life.

What could that possibly feel like? Maybe he felt like a god. Or maybe, somewhere deep down, he felt like he was doing something wrong.

"Don't look so nervous, Naomi."

Naomi blinked as Sensei clapped his notebook shut.

"Just leave it to me, all right? You're not going to fail as long as you do what I tell you. Your victory is basically preordained. No reason to overthink it, really. Just trust me, and follow the instructions in this notebook."

Turning the notebook over in his hands, he showed Naomi its cover once again.

"It's not every day you get a self-help book from the future, right?"

Naomi flinched a little. The words *self-help book* brought to mind some painful recent memories. His recent purchase, *How to Be Decisive*, contained more than eighty pieces of advice, all of which had been no help whatsoever. He'd wasted 2000 yen on that stupid thing.

Perhaps he bore *some* amount of blame for his failure, since he'd been too much of a chicken to act on the book's advice. But come *on!* That stupid book just said *do this* and *do that* without a single word about what the results would be. It was always terrifying to take a risk without any guarantee of a decent outcome, right?

This notebook was different, though.

The *Ultimate Manual* in Sensei's hand was a description of the future. It was offering him a guaranteed, preset path that could only lead to success.

A bit belatedly, Naomi was realizing just how amazing that was. This was *exactly* what he'd been looking for so desperately last week. It was the single greatest self-help book in the entire world.

"So, what should I do first, Sensei?" he asked excitedly, his heart dancing in his chest. He was eager to give this thing a try.

"Right," Sensei said, nodding in a mildly pompous manner. "Start by taking out a book."

"Yes, sir!"

Naomi pushed his phone into his jacket pocket and retrieved a paperback book from his bag. He was always carrying at least one with him.

"Now open it."

More instructions already!

Naomi had put away his phone, so he couldn't respond verbally anymore. Still, he snapped open the book with a sharp, decisive movement, like a fresh recruit carrying out his orders.

"Now drop it."

Again, he executed his instructions faithfully. The book flopped straight to the floor and fell shut. A moment later, the bus swayed slightly, causing the paperback to slide a few feet along the floor.

"Now go pick it up."

This seemed like a pretty involved operation, but he was keeping up so far.

The bus swayed again, and Naomi's book slid further forward. He chased after it hurriedly on his hands and knees, managing to catch it just before it could slide out of reach.

What the hell am I doing?

A moment of self-reflection caused Naomi's faith to waiver. Was this sequence of events really described in that journal? It was hard to see what he could possibly be accomplishing.

The bus swayed again, and Naomi's head smacked into the backside of the person standing in front of him.

"Uh, I'm sorry..." He apologized reflexively as he looked up at the other passenger.

Meeting his gaze from above were the glowing eyes of a ruthless predator—the eyes of a viper sizing up a toad, or a lion contemplating a rabbit.

I was right the first time. She's definitely not the cute type.

As Naomi stepped down off the bus at his stop, he looked over at his classmate.

Given his role as a rabbit, he'd been unable to do anything except quiver fearfully on the ground and await his doom. Accordingly, he'd received a hard slap across the face.

Naomi was *one* of the guilty parties here, so his punishment was probably warranted...but he found it a bit unfair that the true mastermind of the incident had escaped unscathed.

He appealed to his judge and jury's sympathy with a pathetic look of remorse. Ichigyou Ruri shot him a withering glare, then turned and strode off. For a long moment, Naomi just stood there at the bus stop. His left cheek started to sting.

Oh, that hurts. That really hurts...

"Excellent," said Sensei with a nod.

"Excellent?! What was excellent about that?!" Naomi protested angrily. Whatever he'd been doing, it had turned out *horribly*! "She thinks I'm a scumbag now! She probably hates me. Were you reading from the *Ruin Everything Manual* by mistake? What am I supposed to do now, huh?!"

"First, stop freaking out."

Now Sensei was just asking the impossible.

His face calm and composed, the older man wagged a finger chidingly. "All of that was just a necessary bit of groundwork." He pointed dramatically down at the ground.

"Um..." Naomi's voice came out in a squeak. He almost wished it had gone unheard, but the library was deserted and silent today, so it carried just fine.

He was on the second floor of the library, in a corner divided from the rest by partitions. The after-school committee meeting would be starting soon. But for the moment, the only people there were Ichigyou Ruri—the first to arrive—and Naomi, who'd followed her there.

Ruri's eyes moved from her book to Naomi's face.

She wore the same look of scorn he'd seen earlier. Naomi almost thought she might slap him a second time, just to send a message. He wanted nothing more than to turn on his heel and flee. But he *couldn't* do that. It wasn't what the *Ultimate Manual* said would happen.

He just needed to recite his lines. He didn't need to think. It was just like reading from a script, really.

Gathering up all his courage, he managed to speak.

"I'm, uh...sorry about yesterday. You know, the thing that happened on the bus. I was just trying to pick this up for you."

Embarrassed by his wooden delivery, Naomi took out his prop—a bookmark that Ruri had dropped on the bus. It was a colorful little thing with a peacock-feather design. Apparently, it had slipped out from between the pages of her paperback.

In reality, Naomi had picked it up at the bus stop, not on the bus itself. It wasn't responsible for him face-planting into her butt.

In other words, he was lying to her. But Sensei insisted that such "minor details" weren't important. The only thing that mattered was getting results.

"I was looking for that." Ruri rose from her seat quickly, the hostility gone from her face. She stood ramrod straight in front of Naomi for a moment, then bowed her head to him.

"I'm very sorry. I didn't even give you a chance to explain."

It made Naomi feel seriously awkward. He hadn't been

expecting an apology, and he didn't really deserve one.

"Uh, that's okay," he said, flapping his hand in the air. "It never would have happened if I'd just spoken up, you know?"

He knew it sounded plausible enough, though knowing that he had no good reason for bumping into her backside made him embarrassed all over again.

He really, really wanted to end this conversation. Stepping forward, he practically pushed the bookmark into Ruri's hands. She finally raised her head and accepted it.

Ruri looked at the colorful little thing, and then looked Naomi in the eyes. The disgusted look was gone, but she wasn't exactly smiling at him, either. Her face was composed, neutral, and cold—almost like a metal mask.

"Thank you very much."

"Oh, don't worry about it..."

Just as Naomi was handing back the strangely grandmotherly bookmark, a group of other committee members came up the stairs from the second floor. It was a cheerful group, chattering loudly as they approached; unsurprisingly, Kadenokouji Misuzu was among them.

Sensing a good moment to withdraw, Naomi cut off the conversation with Ichigyou as politely as he could.

In all honesty, speaking with her had been kind of intimidating. Much like Misuzu and her friends, Ruri really wasn't the kind of person Naomi had ever interacted with before.

Naomi watched Ruri as she left the school building and

walked off at a steady pace. It looked like she was heading straight home now that the committee meeting was over. Not that he knew her well enough to propose walking home together, of course.

"We've got a long way to go...but you made some progress today. A little, at least."

Naomi thought his heart would jump out of his chest. At some point, Sensei had materialized at his side. These jump scares couldn't be good for his heart.

"Don't get too impatient yet, okay?" Sensei said with a smile, taking out his notebook, the *Ultimate Manual*, with its tantalizing promises of guaranteed results. Sensei held one of its first pages between his fingers as he continued. "Your romance is just getting started."

3.

[April 23RD—WiZ message from the library committee]

NAOMI WAS READING IN HIS BEDROOM when his phone started to vibrate.

There was a WiZ notification on the screen, just as Sensei had predicted. Opening the app, he read the entire message.

"Chairman: For the shelf cleaning on Monday, we're asking you all to bring your own dust cloths. Please let anyone who isn't in the chat know before the end of the weekend."

Naomi furrowed his brow slightly.

A certain someone wasn't in the group, and he was responsible for passing this message to her. But the two of them weren't in contact, really. He didn't have her phone number or her email address.

"How am I supposed to—"

As he turned around, the question half-spoken, he found Sensei ready and waiting for him. The three-legged crow was perched on his arm like a falconer's bird. In its beak, it held a blank white envelope, which it had presumably plucked from Naomi's drawer.

Naomi understood what Sensei was implying.

He didn't have Ruri's email or her phone number, but he did have one means of reaching her. Technically. Although the idea felt *very weird.*

The committee members sat in a circle of desks that faced inward. On the whiteboard in the back of the room, the words *CLEANING DAY* were written in big, bold letters, and someone had added cutesy little stars around them. Naomi guessed they were Misuzu's doing, which ended up being correct. She was the kind of girl you'd expect to do that sort of thing.

Naomi glanced at the girl sitting next to him and tried to picture *her* drawing sparkles on a whiteboard. It was totally impossible.

"Okay, so! As you saw in the message, we're going to be cleaning the shelves today."

The committee chairman started to divide up this sizable task. Soon, everyone began taking out their dust cloths and placing them on top of their tables. As Naomi did the same, he glanced over just as the girl next to him was looking his way.

Their eyes met.

Ichigyou Ruri gave him a small bow of thanks.

Naomi nodded back at her and felt himself relax a little. Apparently the letter he'd written on Friday had made it to her house in time.

Yes, he'd sent a letter. An actual, physical letter. Through the mail.

It was a pretty convenient system when you thought about it—you could send anyone a message as long as you knew where they lived. But Naomi had only taken advantage of it a handful of times in his entire life. And writing that letter in particular had been genuinely nerve-racking.

If he'd been writing to an old friend, it probably wouldn't have been so bad. But he was writing to a *girl*, specifically to one he was trying to get closer to. Surely his anxiety was understandable.

In the end, he'd crumpled up seven failed drafts before finally approving his eighth try—a totally bland, businesslike message. Sensei had indicated that this was the correct approach. Naomi had paid a bit extra to expedite the letter. It had clearly gotten there on time, so that was 360 yen well spent.

Once everyone had their assignments, the library committee got to work cleaning. Ruri and Naomi didn't really strike up a conversation; for the most part, they just ran their dust cloths silently along their assigned shelves.

When Naomi got home that day and checked the mail, he found that a letter addressed to him had arrived. It was a plain, standard envelope, with no decorations of any kind. But on the back was the name Ichigyou Ruri.

Hurrying back to his room, Naomi carefully opened the envelope with a pair of scissors. The letter that emerged was a simple handwritten note: *Thank you for passing on the message.*

The sight of it made him chuckle. Something about this sincere, one-sentence letter was oddly funny. He found himself picturing her sending it—methodically writing out the words, sealing the envelope, and placing it into the mailbox.

He tried to visualize her at that specific moment. Somehow, he doubted she'd been smiling. She'd probably dropped it in there with that flat, neutral expression of hers, like she was mailing in a warranty card or something.

The mental image made Naomi chuckle again.

4.

[May 6TH—Desk duty at the library]

RURI AND NAOMI SAT next to each other behind the checkout desk, reading their books.

The committee members on desk duty were expected to man the library during their lunch period and after school. They were there to process check-outs and returns, keep the shelves organized, post any new announcements on the walls, and repair slightly damaged books.

However, Nishiki High didn't have that big a collection in the first place, and there usually wasn't enough work to fill the entire shift. Unless there was some sort of special event going on, the people on duty had plenty of time to goof off.

Naomi shot a quick glance to the girl next to him. Ruri appeared to be totally engrossed in her book. He was reading too, so he wasn't about to complain or anything. The total lack of conversation was starting to feel a little awkward, though.

They were both avid readers. Surely there were plenty of things they *could* chat about. A simple question like "What are you reading?" would have been enough to kick things off. Naomi had read plenty of interesting books in all sorts of genres; if he knew what kind of book she was reading, he'd probably be able to keep the conversation going for quite some time.

Of course, taking that first step was never as easy as it sounded. Otherwise, he never would have resorted to buying some rip-off self-help book.

At the moment, the only thing he knew for sure was the color of the book cover Ruri was using.

Ten minutes passed that way, as Naomi tried to psych himself up to say something. But then Ruri closed her book, got up, and started tidying the shelves. They couldn't leave the checkout counter unmanned, so Naomi couldn't follow.

With a very quiet little sigh, he turned back to his own book. Thanks to his less-than-cheerful mood, he was finding it hard to focus on the story.

"Oh, that *sucks*, dude!"

Naomi jumped a little in his seat.

Someone was talking in the library, and their voice was *way* too loud. The sudden burst of sound had rattled him. Looking nervously in the direction it had come from, he saw a pair of third-year boys sitting in the browsing area.

"Yeah, no kidding. And then that jerk Nishiyama just went home."

"What a moron!"

This wasn't going to be a one-off thing, apparently. The volume of their voices was slightly lower than it had been at first, but it was still far too loud for the library. To make matters worse, the voices were joined by the sound of a plastic bag being torn open.

Keeping his head down, Naomi glanced over. The two older boys were eating packaged bread from the school store in the browsing area. Of *course*, there was no eating or drinking allowed in the library. And it was the committee members' job to enforce those rules.

Naomi tried to picture himself scolding those two and immediately winced. Averting his eyes, he returned his focus to the pages of his book. Nothing had even happened yet, but he could feel himself physically cowering.

Those guys had been at this school for much longer than him.

They knew how things really worked around here, and they obviously thought they could behave any way they pleased. How was he supposed to reason with people like that?

He *wanted* to tell them off. Of course he did. He wanted to make them put their food away. He wanted to say, *Hey, you're going to get the books dirty*, or something. No one wanted a bunch of food stains on their library books, right?

Naomi lowered his face a little further.

Why do I have to be so pathetic?

"Please don't eat or drink in the library. It's not allowed."

Naomi jerked his head up in surprise. Ruri was standing right next to the two older boys, looking down at them coolly.

"Oh, right. Sorry about that."

The two students put their food away without protest. After watching them do so, Ruri offered a small bow and a few polite words, then returned to sorting the shelves.

Naomi just looked on, his mouth hanging partially open. This ordinary girl had suddenly become an all-powerful superhero.

By the time they left school, Horigawa Street was glowing orange in the light of the setting sun.

There was a city bus stop just outside the gates of Nishiki High that many of the students used to commute. Ichigyou Ruri was one of them, so she lined up at the stop as usual.

"Okay, then. I'll see you later."

As Naomi tried to say goodbye, Ruri gave him a strange look. "Weren't you on the same bus as me the other day?"

"Oh. Yeah, true."

"I assumed your house was in the same direction as mine."

"Uh, well, I was..."

Naomi felt a shiver run down his spine. Ruri probably thought of this as an innocent question, but he couldn't help feeling like he was being interrogated. If he slipped up now, only the death penalty awaited him.

And of course, the bus was here, just to add some time pressure to the equation. It had already come to a stop and opened its doors. He had to answer *now*.

"I w-was actually heading to the Kita Library that day. It's a little far away, but it's the only branch around here that gets *Deduction Magazine*."

Naomi ended up spitting the words out a bit too rapidly. It made him want to cringe. If *he* were a girl, he definitely wouldn't want to date this big an idiot.

"Ah, I see." With those flat words, Ichigyou stepped up onto the bus. But just as the doors were closing, she added one additional comment.

"I read it there every month, too."

The doors slid shut, and the bus pulled away.

Naomi's expression grew a little brighter as he watched it go. All in all, that had gone pretty well. He'd spoken with Ruri. He'd talked to her about reading, specifically. He'd even found out they read the same magazine. And he'd carried out his mission.

Once the bus had safely disappeared from view, Naomi took a note out of his pocket. On the small square of paper, he'd written down the exact conversation they'd just had in advance.

Thank God for the Ultimate Manual...

Naomi looked up and off to one side. Sensei was standing on the top of a building across the street with that three-legged crow perched on his arm.

Naomi offered him a small wave. It was a little embarrassing, but he wanted to convey that he'd succeeded.

Sensei responded with a thumbs-up.

5.

IRON, NAOMI CHANTED.

He didn't speak the word out loud, but he repeated it in his mind many, many times. The more he repeated it, however, the more counterproductive it felt. The word *iron* wasn't iron itself, after all—it was just a pair of syllables.

Giving up on the word, he decided to visualize the substance instead. He gripped his gloved right hand's wrist with his left hand to steady it. He sensed that keeping it perfectly still might improve the results somehow.

With renewed focus, he mentally pictured a piece of iron. Sensei had told him not to close his eyes; he had to learn how to work with them open, apparently. The glove started to tremble slightly. Its vague, indeterminate form pulsed against his fingers. It felt a bit like the first tremors before an earthquake.

Naomi focused.

He pictured the shape, the weight, the color—the real, concrete properties of matter.

And then, he closed his hand forcefully.

His glove abruptly stopped quivering. The little tremors dissipated. All of a sudden, he realized he was holding something heavy.

Slowly, he opened his hand. There was a small iron ball sitting in his palm, shiny enough to reflect Naomi's face.

"Sensei! Sensei!"

Naomi rushed over to his teacher, who was sitting on a log nearby. He'd been reviewing some sort of data for a while and hadn't been paying attention. Looking over the fruits of Naomi's labor, he murmured, "Hmm, look at that."

"This is incredible! Look, it's iron! It's real iron!"

"That it is."

Sensei made a circle with his fingers and peered at the ball through it. It was a gesture he made on a regular basis. He'd explained that he could call up all sorts of information displays this way.

"Nice and dense, too. Not many impurities..."

Naomi couldn't suppress a smug chuckle of satisfaction at that assessment. He'd worked hard to pull this off. Harder than Sensei knew, in fact.

In the three weeks since they'd met, Naomi had practiced with the glove first thing in the morning every day. These training sessions with Sensei were intense and difficult and rarely earned him any praise. He'd been eager to surprise the man at least once, so he'd started practicing in his bedroom late into the night.

Naomi pictured the periodic table poster hanging in his room. Fe was atomic number 26, and its density was relatively high. Creating it had proven more difficult than he'd imagined, but after ten long days of solo practice, he'd finally managed to create it from scratch all on his own.

"This is pretty amazing, right? Don't you think?" he asked Sensei, grinning happily. He felt like he deserved a few more compliments for pulling this off, in all honesty.

Sensei responded with a warm smile and by pointing into the air. Naomi looked up to see dozens of giant shiny iron balls floating in the sky—and then, suddenly, they shot down directly at him.

"Eeeek!"

I'm dead!

Throwing his arms over his head, Naomi huddled against the ground. There was no way he could ward off those enormous balls of iron. He was going to die.

Just as that thought crossed his mind, the barrage of iron balls hit the ground without a sound. They piled up there for a moment, and then disappeared all at once.

Oh. Right...

"They're only illusions, kid. I told you I can't interact with this world, didn't I?" With a perfectly serious expression on his face, Sensei approached his cowering pupil.

"Next time, *deal with it* instead of freaking out. Make a nice thick ceiling for yourself, or dig a tunnel into the ground.

Whatever. There's all sorts of options."

"I can't just improvise something on the spur of the moment!"

"Oh? You can't?" Sensei's voice dropped in tone. It was suddenly almost hostile. "Is that what you're going to say when her life depends on it?"

Naomi looked up at Sensei's face. He could feel those words, colder and heavier than iron, pressing down on his shoulders.

Sensei was talking about the *incident*—the bolt of lightning that would hit the riverbank, claiming Ruri's life, and their attempt to save her from that fate.

Failure wasn't an option. They'd only have one chance.

"No matter how precisely we recreate the original events, my presence here *will* have an impact," Sensei continued. "There's no telling whether the accident will occur exactly as recorded. We can try our best, but there are no guarantees."

Sensei paused to look Naomi straight in the eye.

"That's why you need to be capable of protecting her, no matter what happens. Even if things take a totally unexpected turn, you need to find some way to succeed. And that means you need to become capable of doing *anything*."

Fighting the urge to avert his eyes, Naomi let the words wash over him. He needed to be capable of *anything*? Did this man expect him to become some kind of god?

"The God Hand is powerful enough to make that possible, at least in theory."

Naomi already knew that. Sensei had explained the glove's potential when he gave it to him, how it could rewrite the fabric of the world. Once you learned how to use it, you could do almost anything. It did seem almost divine.

In other words, if he fell short—

"It all depends on how *you* use it." Sensei gave him the answer unprompted. Unable to endure his steady gaze, Naomi looked away. He'd finally bent under the pressure.

His eyes, searching for something else to focus on, settled on his own hand. A vague sense of anxiety was bubbling up inside him, growing larger by the second.

Can I really pull this off?

He had a magic glove that could do anything, and the best he could manage with it was creating a little ball of iron. Was he really capable of playing his role competently?

It felt like there was a great weight pressing down on his heart. This was a very familiar feeling. His subconscious mind was telling him it was time to run—to get off the path he was on before the moment of truth arrived.

To the best of his ability, Naomi avoided taking risks. He didn't like challenging himself unless the outcome was predictable. These were the rules he'd lived by for fifteen years, and they still bound him in place. He couldn't just reinvent himself all of sudden. He'd spent his middle school years avoiding everything that made him uncomfortable; he wasn't going to shake that habit in a day.

And yet—

He *had* gone out and bought himself that book, hoping he could change.

There was a pile of books sitting on Naomi's desk in his bedroom. They were thicker and larger than his usual paperbacks—these were introductory texts and reference books for various scientific fields.

Naomi enjoyed studying. When you put more effort in, you would reliably be rewarded for it. It was one of the few things he could focus on without getting anxious.

So, he'd picked up a habit of studying when he was feeling nervous. He could just hit the books until his fears faded. It was his only real coping method, and in the face of this new dilemma, he turned to it once again.

First, he worked his way through a chapter of a physics text. Then he switched over to a chemistry book. He decided to skip biology; living things were supposedly too complex to mess with, after all.

In a corner of his mind, Sensei's words of advice played on a constant loop.

"The most important thing you can do is foster your power of imagination."

Putting down his book, Naomi stepped out onto his balcony. It was better to be out here, in case he screwed things up. Squatting down on the concrete in his sandals, he tensed his gloved hand in anticipation.

"Convince your mind that you can make iron in the blink of an eye, and then demonstrate to yourself that it's true."

Air began to turn to metal in the palm of his hand.

I can do this. I can do this in a second. It's easy, he repeated to himself, but the process still moved slowly.

Come on! Faster! Faster! he thought impatiently.

The half-completed ball of iron suddenly broke down into a kind of goo. It popped like a balloon, sending glops of the stuff flying off in all directions.

"Ew!"

Naomi piled a new stack of reference material on his desk. He had architecture texts, interior design books, and even a catalog from a fancy furniture store over by Shijo-Karasuma.

"Don't assume anything's impossible. Shrug off your doubts. Let your imagination soar."

After flipping through the catalog for a while, Naomi picked a specific page, cut it out with a pair of scissors, and taped it to his wall. It was a listing for a desk with the staggering price tag of nearly 40,000 yen. Its design was quite simple; it had metal pipes for legs and a simple drawer.

This shouldn't be too hard, right?

Naomi placed his right hand on the surface of his own desk, which was a simple slab of wood built into his closet space. He'd added on some shelves later to give it a bit more storage space.

He didn't exactly *dislike* this desk. But if he was going to exhaust himself practicing with the God Hand, it couldn't hurt to improve his furniture a bit while he was at it.

Naomi visualized, as best he could, that bewilderingly expensive desk.

"Believe that anything is possible. Tell yourself you're a wizard from a fantasy novel."

I'm a wizard, damn it. I'm a wizard!

The desk began to change form. The wood distorted and wriggled. With all his willpower, he pulled it into a brand-new shape.

The result resembled an avant-garde abstract art monstrosity. A mass of wood, having lost its purpose, stared resentfully at its creator with distorted, lumpy eyes.

Naomi piled up yet another stack of books. This time, he balanced them on top of the lid that partially covered his bathtub. Each book was sealed inside a Ziploc bag to protect it from the moisture. It was a trick he'd picked up some time ago.

"You can shape everything exactly as you want it. Give the world its marching orders!"

As he soaked in the tub, Naomi flipped through another book on physics, reviewing the basic concepts: the properties of matter, heat, entropy, and energy.

After finishing his chapter, he stepped out into the rinsing area. It felt kind of weird to be wearing just a glove while otherwise totally naked, but he didn't have much choice.

He started off by washing his hair with soap and water normally. But then, instead of turning on the shower, he positioned his right hand directly over his head.

Visualizing a bath attendant pouring water from a bucket, he muttered the word "shower" to himself.

"Agh! That's cold!"

Ice-cold water rained down on him from the glove. He jumped to his feet and stomped angrily on the ground. *Hot water! I want hot water, dammit!*

"Gaaah! Hot! Hot!"

This time, he hit himself with a blast of scalding water that sent him dancing across the bathroom. Apparently, he only had two output settings: zero degrees Celsius or 100.

Hadn't Sensei told him water was supposed to be easy? Why did adults have to *lie* about everything?

In his frustration, he ended up practicing over and over until he finally managed to produce water at a perfect 42 degrees Celsius.

When he finally emerged from the bathroom after spending nearly two hours on this project, his mom grinned and asked if he had a crush on someone. She seemed to assume he'd been grooming himself in there.

Naomi couldn't explain, of course, so the only retort he could think of was a sulky "leave me alone."

There was a calendar hanging from a tree branch, turned to the month of May. Many of the days had already been crossed off.

Naomi looked back to his own hand with its glowing blue glove. He remembered all the hours he'd spent practicing with this thing. And with all the concentration he could muster, he squeezed his hand shut.

"Raaah!"

The glove trembled briefly.

There was something resting in his palm now—something with a bit of heft to it.

Slowly, he opened his hand.

"How's that?"

Sensei made a ring with his fingers and peered down at the object. "Looks like copper, all right."

Cu was 29th on the periodic table. It was only a little heavier than iron, but it had taken him quite a while to create it.

"Hey, we've still got time. Not *that* much of it, but some. Don't get discouraged," Sensei said, trying to counter the dejection that Naomi was clearly projecting.

Naomi hung his head slightly, squeezing the little ball of copper. There wasn't much time left at all—that was the cold, hard truth.

He felt sorry for himself for a nice long moment...until he finally thought to check the time.

"Oh crap, I've got to go!" As important as this training was, he couldn't start missing school, either.

"Hey, hold on," shouted Sensei as he turned to run off. "You've got something coming up today, remember?"

6.

[May 17th—After school—Shelf-sorting duty]

THE TALL BOOKSHELVES TOWERED overhead like a castle rampart. Ichigyou Ruri stood before them with a small cart full of books at her side.

Having put away the books on the lower shelves, she was now contemplating the next stage of her job. The very top shelves were too tall for most people to reach; the library had a few three-level stepladders for accessing them.

Ruri stepped cautiously onto the first step of her stepladder with a single book in her arms. Rather than walking right up like most people would, she placed her other foot carefully on the first step as well.

There was a faint rattling sound. Were her legs shaking, or was it the stepladder? Maybe both.

Slowly, Ruri brought her right foot onto the second step, then followed with her left.

By the time she reached the third step, her face was blank, and her eyes were focused entirely on the gap in the bookshelf. She looked like a primitive robot, fixated solely on a single aspect of its task.

Gently, she pushed the book back into its space and, with her task complete, that blank look gave way to something a bit more human. She suddenly noticed the rest of the world around her.

Her gaze fell toward the floor.

Instantly, her face went pale. Then, she went limp.

"Unh..."

With a small groan, she tumbled from the top of the stepladder—which was only about eighty centimeters off the ground.

"Gah!"

Naomi let out a frog-like croak as he absorbed the impact.

He'd fantasized about catching her in his arms, but that just wasn't realistic. He didn't have the necessary physique; realistically, the best he could do was act as a shock-absorbing mat.

Somehow, he'd never imagined a girl would feel this *heavy* lying on top of him. But, well, he couldn't expect reality to be like fiction.

A while later, Ruri was lying on the sofa in the library's cramped side room.

This place was a bit of a storage area, but also served as a break room. There were crammed steel shelves against the walls, overflowing with files and documents. In between the random piles of unopened cardboard boxes, someone had also deposited an old set of sofas; they were probably leftovers from some office renovation.

Naomi had helped Ruri in here and was waiting for her to recover. The top half of her face was hidden underneath a damp handkerchief.

Her breathing seemed a little shallow. Naomi could see her mouth moving slightly. After a moment, he realized he was staring at it and jerked his eyes away.

"I'm not good with heights," Ruri groaned softly.

That seemed like an understatement, considering she'd only been less than a meter above the ground. If someone ever took this girl up to the observation deck of the Kyoto Tower, she might just drop dead on the spot.

"Everyone has their weaknesses," Naomi said gently. "From now on, why don't I put back all the books on the top shelves?"

"All right," Ruri replied, pushing herself up to a sitting position. "I'll focus on the bottom shelves, then."

Naomi really thought she should rest a little longer. He found himself starting to reach out toward her. But he didn't have the guts to touch her, so he ended up pulling his hand back indecisively.

"The bottom shelves have a lot of oversized books. Those things are really heavy. I'll do them, too."

"I'll take the middle shelves, then."

Naomi found himself looking for a reason to argue, but couldn't find any. "Okay, that works."

Ruri nodded and reached out for the juice pack Naomi had bought her from the vending machines in the school store. "Thank you for this, by the way."

She took a long, *long* drink of juice through the straw for what felt like thirty seconds straight. *She must have good lung capacity*, Naomi thought.

Leaning back in the chair in his room, Naomi gazed absently at his smartphone screen.

"Splitting up the job that way was incredibly inefficient," said Sensei from somewhere above him. He'd popped up in Naomi's room a little earlier, as suddenly as always. "First, we had to sort out the middle shelf books from all the others. And I wasted tons of time going up and down that ladder constantly. But it forced us to communicate. We *had* to work together to get it done, you see? Looking back on it now, I think that was a turning point."

"Yowch!"

Out of nowhere, the crow attacked Naomi. Its three legs unleashed a fearsome barrage of kicks at his head.

"Are you listening?"

"Sorry! Wasn't paying attention! Gah!"

Naomi's apology didn't halt the assault. He had to drop his phone to protect his head.

"What are you smirking about, anyway?" Bending down, Sensei examined the screen of the fallen phone.

"I wasn't smirking," Naomi protested, but it was too late now.

The screen was displaying his WiZ friends list, which now contained the name *Ichigyou Ruri*.

He'd finally managed to add her today.

Ruri had only gotten her first smartphone upon entering high school, and she didn't have much of an interest in it. She'd been carrying it around without really using it. Now that they were talking more, Naomi had volunteered to help her get the hang of it; while teaching her how to use WiZ, he'd showed her how to add him as her first friend.

Naomi was happy to have her name in his phone. And it was even better knowing that *his* name was the only one in *hers*. He couldn't have described exactly what he was feeling, but it was definitely nice.

Despite his protests, he probably *had* been smirking. But he'd worked hard for a solid month to get this far. He felt like he'd earned the right.

Looking up at Sensei, he found the man was smiling.

"Hey, good for you."

It was rare to get that kind of encouragement from this man. Naomi's mood was suddenly downright buoyant.

"It's all thanks to you, Sensei!"

This was true, of course. Naomi was entirely reliant on that *Ultimate Manual*. As long as he followed its descriptions to the letter, he would always get the results that it described. A few weeks ago, he could barely have spoken to Ruri, and now he had her as a contact in his phone. That would have been impossible without Sensei's help.

Things weren't so rosy when it came to the God Hand. His effort wasn't producing predictable results. He was still deeply anxious about whether he'd be able to play his role when the time came.

But this part was different. He was making steady progress. As long as he carried out his instructions to the letter, he would keep getting closer to Ruri.

Sensei told him what to do, and he played the role he'd been assigned. All he was doing was following orders, really.

But still...this was a victory they'd won *together*. It made him really happy.

"What do we do next?" Naomi asked excitedly as he bent down to pick up his phone.

"We keep at it," said Sensei with a smile. "We do what we need to do."

For once, it felt like they were on the same page.

"Try to calm down, though. I don't want you getting impatient on me." Sensei opened his notebook and began flipping through it. That battered old thing had the future inside it—the future as it was meant to be. It was kind of awe-inspiring.

"As long as you keep this up, it's going to work out in the end. You've got a cheat sheet from the future, remember? You're guaranteed to win her over."

Despite Sensei's words of caution, the words *win her over* got Naomi's blood pumping a little faster.

It was hard not to be impatient. Soon, he was going to have his first girlfriend *ever*.

7.

NAOMI WATCHED as the words *June 25th* were scrawled on the library's whiteboard. It was a date about three weeks in the future.

The chairman continued writing, adding four words in large letters: *Charity Used Book Sale*.

"The book sale is our single biggest event of the year. Anyone heard of it before?"

A number of hands went up around the room, including Ruri's; Naomi held his hand up hesitantly a moment later. Maybe one-third of the committee members knew about the sale, from the look of things.

"Yeah, that seems about right. It's not really a big event." The chairman didn't seem particularly upset by this, fortunately.

"Starting today, we're going to be collecting used books to sell on the 25th. We'll set up donation boxes in the library and the classrooms and ask everyone to donate whatever they can. Of course, we don't want anything too beaten up..."

Once the basic explanation was complete, they began dividing the committee up into teams, each with different responsibilities. People moved around the room seemingly at random, but a large group quickly formed around Kadenokouji Misuzu.

At one point in the discussion, she'd casually dropped the following remark: "Sometimes the salesclerks dress up in cute outfits for stuff like this, right?"

It had been intended as an offhand comment, but a bunch of committee members had instantly latched on to it and were getting excited. Certain students began muttering the words *salesgirls* and *cosplay* and rejoined the meeting with intense focus.

Naomi had no intention of joining that group, but he did feel a small spark of excitement. Any costume Misuzu wore would look adorable by default, and it would probably attract plenty of customers to the sale, too.

Fighting against the current, Misuzu pushed her way over to Ruri.

"You should dress up too, Ru!"

Naomi was astonished at the mere suggestion. *She'll never agree to that in a million years...* This was Ichigyou Ruri they were talking about, after all. He couldn't think of anyone *less* likely to indulge in cosplay.

That wasn't to say she couldn't pull it off, of course. There were probably some options that would suit her very well. The first idea to pop into Naomi's head was Jadis, the White Witch from the Chronicles of Narnia, accompanied by her loyal polar bear. She was a witch who wielded ice as a weapon and took pleasure in executing her enemies. It felt like a perfect fit...not that he was *ever* going to say so.

"I don't think so," said Ruri, predictably enough. "Also, didn't I tell you to cut that out?"

"Cut what out?"

"The *Ru* thing."

"Hmm. Okay. How about I call you Ruru?"

"That's even worse."

"Rurine?"

"No."

"Rudy Rutabaga?"

"Excuse me?"

Misuzu seemed determined to draw Ruri out of her shell for whatever reason, but it was clearly an uphill battle. The wall of ice showed no sign of thawing.

Naomi was only a spectator, but the conversation made him increasingly nervous. Couldn't she try to be a *little* more receptive? Misuzu was obviously trying to make friends.

Then again, Ruri was clearly all right on her own. She spent most of her free time reading in the classroom and seemed to prefer being left alone. It was the same in the committee meetings—she was diligent about her duties, but never struck up conversations with anyone.

The girl wasn't a team player *at all*, and she seemed to know that about herself.

But wasn't that going to be a problem?

Sensei's instructions from that morning flashed back through Naomi's head.

"The used book sale in June is going to be a big event for us, too," Sensei said, gesturing at the calendar hanging from the tree branch.

"What do I need to do?"

"At the moment, things are heading in the right direction. If you get off track, I'll let you know. For right now, just focus on getting books for that sale. Get as many as you *possibly* can. That's all I want you thinking about."

Naomi nodded easily. It sounded simple enough—he just had to do his normal committee job.

Naomi wrote his name on the whiteboard. Ruri was right next to him, doing the same. Rather than the flashier groups like Costumes or Publicity, they'd both chosen the least exciting option: the Book Collection team. After what Sensei had told him, Naomi had fully expected this to happen.

He'd actually been a little worried when Misuzu tried to physically drag Ruri into the Costumes group. But in the end, events had followed their proper course.

The next day, the two of them placed a donation box in their classroom and encouraged everyone to donate books.

Now he had to do everything he could to find more.

8.

HOMEROOM ENDED, and the students flowed out of the classroom.

As the noise died down, Naomi opened the lid of the donation box. Ruri was at his side and peered down into it with him. There were two books sitting at the bottom.

Frowning, Naomi looked over at the blackboard. The date written there was proof that a full week had passed. Two books over five school days meant they were getting a whole 0.4 donations per day.

"Well," he said with an awkward little smile, "I guess they did say we shouldn't expect too much..."

The chairman had described the results from recent years, so Naomi hadn't been expecting anything too amazing. Still, this was a bit more depressing than he'd expected it would be.

This definitely wasn't good enough, was it?

Sensei had told him to get as many books as he possibly could. Two donations wasn't close to enough. At this rate, they might diverge from the events recorded in the *Ultimate Manual*.

Naomi wasn't sure what to do, though. He couldn't *force* his classmates to donate books. He was willing to put the effort in, but he didn't know how.

"Katagaki-san."

Looking over, he saw that Ruri was still staring down into the box with a serious look on her face.

"We're on the Book Collection team, correct?" The look in her eyes was beyond serious. Was she actually a little angry?

"Our job is to collect books. We should pursue that goal any way we can. We might not succeed, but there's no excuse for not *trying*."

"Yeah. You're right."

Naomi was a little startled at first, but maybe he shouldn't have been. Ruri didn't go out of her way to talk to the other committee members, true. But when it came to her actual responsibilities, she took them extremely seriously.

"Let's do everything we can," Ruri said, clutching her hands into fists.

They shared a common goal. That was good. But Naomi wasn't particularly confident he could keep up with her.

Their avenues for action were limited, but they fully pursued every one that came to mind.

First, they got permission to place a new donation box in

the faculty lounge, hoping they could guilt some teachers into supporting their students. Of course, the adults were all busy people, so they couldn't expect much.

Next, Ruri hit on the idea of standing in the hallways at lunch holding donation boxes in their arms and calling out to people passing by. It wasn't a bad idea in theory, but people rarely walked around with used books they were willing to donate. Still, there was a chance it would at least increase awareness of the donation drive, so they kept at it. Naomi found the process deeply embarrassing, but when he saw Ruri bowing her head to everyone who walked by, he *had* to follow suit.

Eventually, they even left the school grounds entirely and asked for permission to place a donation box at the nearest community center. The old man at the front desk there didn't like the idea, but they begged and pleaded at great length. At one point, another staff member came by and said it sounded fine to him, but then they realized he thought the boxes were for recycling old newspapers. They never did manage to get approval.

And as they pursued these dead ends, the clock ticked ruthlessly forward.

Naomi picked up an eraser. Wiping away the numbers on the whiteboard, he wrote new ones: *37 books collected—3 days remaining.*

He frowned as he considered the numbers. So did Ruri, standing beside him.

Things were not looking good.

"Hey, that's not a bad haul, really," called the chairman from behind them with a casual tone. "Try to bring a couple from home to pad things out a little, okay? It should be enough." With a wave, he left the room—presumably headed home.

A part of Naomi thought he wasn't taking this seriously enough. But it was the other way around, wasn't it? He was taking it way *too* seriously. Collecting lots of books was a purely personal goal for him, with a totally selfish motivation. He wanted to follow Sensei's instructions to the letter. He *wanted* to start dating Ruri.

Without that tantalizing possibility on the horizon, he wouldn't have gotten so worked up about this either. It wouldn't be fair of him to expect the other committee members to put in the same effort.

That said...

Naomi glanced over at Ruri. She was still staring at the numbers on the blackboard with a deadly serious look on her face.

She would have put the effort in no matter what. Even if he hadn't helped her and she'd been forced to do it all alone, she would still have gone out there, bowed her head to everyone, and scraped together all the books she could.

He *knew* it was true. That was just the kind of person Ruri was.

He had to admire her for it.

"Hmm..."

Ruri nodded to herself abruptly and looked over at Naomi. His heart beat a little faster as their eyes met.

"All right. I have an idea."

After a two-minute walk from the bus stop, Ruri and Naomi approached a plot of land bordered by an absolutely antique-looking wooden wall. Ruri strode confidently alongside it, and Naomi followed close behind.

A large building came into view on the property. It was a splendid old mansion, the kind of place that looked like it might charge admission.

"Come on in," said Ruri as she opened the wooden front gate. Looking around nervously, Naomi followed her as she stepped onto the grounds.

Ruri's home was located on a quiet residential corner in the Shimogamo district, a bit upstream along the Kamo River. There was a city-run botanical garden close nearby, and the mountains that surrounded the Kyoto Basin were noticeably closer here. There were few stores or businesses around, and no library at all, so Naomi rarely visited the area.

The house itself was a large wooden building that really did look like something out of a period TV show. If he hadn't known better, Naomi would have assumed it was some sort of historical landmark. It was that impressive.

After double-checking to make sure there wasn't anyone taking tickets, he hurried along after Ruri. She headed past the main building, toward the back of the spacious lot it sat on.

With a small buzz, the yellow light of incandescent bulbs cut through the darkness. Naomi swallowed as he stepped up the creaking wooden stairs.

He'd walked up into a miniature library.

Ruri had taken him to an old storage building in the corner of her backyard. The first floor had been filled with piles of random boxes, but the attic-like second floor was *completely lined* with wooden bookcases.

Apart from the windowed wooden door that led outside, every single inch of wall was covered with built-in shelves that were packed with books. And even that wasn't enough storage space for the whole collection; the floor was half hidden under piles of dusty tomes.

"These are the books my grandfather collected before he passed away," said Ruri calmly. "He just picked up anything that caught his eye, so I don't think any of them are particularly valuable."

The words didn't fully register with Naomi. The sheer number of old books he was looking at was too much for him to process. A wonderful flood of information washed over him, and his brain threatened to overheat.

Moving a bit unsteadily, he headed over to a nearby shelf and squatted down in front of it. One by one, he studied the spines of the books on the lowest shelf. There were some surprisingly recent books but also many clearly older ones. Just at a glance, he saw novels, works of philosophy, map collections, and reference books. Everything was jumbled up in a chaotic, random mess; and of course, none of them had call numbers on the spine. These were wild books, unlike the domesticated varieties you'd find in a library. They'd been stuffed into these shelves at random.

"Wow."

He hadn't intended to say anything. But there was genuine excitement swelling up inside his chest, and he couldn't hold it down. For someone like Naomi, this was basically a dragon's treasure hoard.

"I guess you grew up reading these books, Ichigyou-san..."

After voicing this thought, Naomi realized it was kind of an embarrassing line. He avoided looking over at Ruri rather than risk seeing her reaction.

"I'd like to donate these books to the school sale."

Naomi blinked and turned toward her, forgetting all about his previous concern.

"I thought it might be a little strange for one person to bring this many books. But I really want to do everything I can."

"Uh, are you sure?" Naomi asked.

He wasn't so sure about the idea, personally. This was his very first visit to this room, but these books already looked like priceless treasures to him. Even if none of them had monetary value, they were clearly precious in other ways.

These were mementos of her departed grandfather, after all. They were a part of her family's history. They were part of *her* history.

"Doesn't this collection mean a lot to you? Do you really want to get rid of them?"

As he spoke those words, Naomi found himself a bit perplexed by his own behavior. He was supposed to be collecting as many books as possible, but here he was, trying to discourage her from donating them.

He knew why, of course. Naomi was a booklover to his core, and a selfish part of him couldn't help but feel it was *wrong* to give a whole collection away.

"I am a little sad to lose them, I suppose..." With a gentle smile, Ruri pulled a book off a nearby shelf. Running her hand over the top of it, she sent a small cloud of dust flying—it caught the light of a hanging lightbulb for a moment before disappearing.

"But I'll never finish reading all these by myself." She paused to look all around her, taking in the entire massive hoard. "I know my grandfather wouldn't have hesitated to donate his old books. And more importantly, a book's meant to be *read*, don't you think?"

Ruri smiled again as she spoke those final words. That was enough to convince Naomi. He could tell she loved books as much as he did. That was what mattered, more than her words themselves. They had to get these hibernating books into the hands of people who would read them.

Meeting her gaze, he nodded firmly. Now that the decision was final, he was eager to get started.

"Okay, then. How the heck do we get them to school?"

Let's carry them ourselves, Ruri had suggested.

They trudged slowly down the dirt road that ran alongside the Kamo River, pushing a big metal handcart. Their sluggish pace wasn't a deliberate choice on their part; they'd gotten greedy and overloaded the cart. Even so, this load was less than one-tenth of the contents of that library.

They'd considered hiring a delivery service at first, but given the number of books, it would have been a *very* expensive job. Two high schoolers couldn't afford that kind of thing. After some uncertainty, they'd settled on the most basic and primitive method of all: hauling them to school a bit at a time over a bunch of trips.

It was about six kilometers from Ruri's house in Shimogamo to Nishiki High, far enough that they'd normally take a bus to get there. Walking briskly, the trip might take a little over an hour on foot... But, dragging a heavy cart along with them, it was probably going to take twice as long.

Naomi found himself doing a little rough mental math. The used book sale was three days away; after today, they'd have two more days to move the books. They could probably manage one round trip after school per day, for a total of three trips. But that wasn't going to be enough to get all the books to school.

Shaking his head, he gripped the rusted metal handle of the handcart a bit more firmly and pushed it stubbornly forward. Ruri was walking in back, pushing from behind. They'd found this thing in the storage building too, and it was a bit of an antique itself; every push forward made its boards squeak and groan. He was getting kind of worried that the bottom might fall out.

Dropping down onto the bench on the riverbank, Naomi

finally managed to catch his breath. They were about halfway to school, but they both *really* needed a break.

Taking an already soggy handkerchief from his pocket, Naomi wiped the sweat off his face as best he could. It *was* late June—summer was sneaking up on them again.

He glanced over at Ruri, who was gulping down mineral water from a plastic bottle. Ultra-Hard Cave Water was the last thing he would have chosen from that vending machine, but for some reason her choice didn't surprise him.

Ruri looked just as sweaty as Naomi felt. Since she was only helping out from behind, she could have gotten away with slacking off a little, but he knew by now that taking it easy wasn't in her nature.

It'd been two and a half months now since they joined the library committee together. Maybe he'd gotten to know her a *little* better in that time.

"By the way, Katagaki-san," she said, turning to look at him, "what kind of books do you like?"

"U-uh..."

She's making small talk now?!

This *was* small talk, right? It had to be. He just had to come up with a reasonable reply, then. He liked all sorts of books. If he wanted to, he could have rattled off a dozen titles and then talked about every one of them at great length.

His conscious mind held him back, though. He caught his hand automatically moving toward his back pocket, but he stopped it. There was no note in there today, no cheat sheet for this one. This was a question *he didn't know about in advance*.

He was sweating again, and it wasn't just from the heat. He'd gotten careless, assuming nothing would happen today. Sensei hadn't warned him, after all.

They were still doing their early-morning training, so he saw Sensei every day. But the man had seemed preoccupied lately. While Naomi practiced, he'd spend the entire session glaring at maps and numbers that floated in midair. The day of the accident was approaching; maybe he was busy planning their strategy for that.

Naomi had gotten more and more comfortable with their peculiar arrangement. At first he'd been nervous and pestered Sensei constantly about the day's events...but the man always warned him when something big was coming up, so he'd stopped bothering. Naomi hadn't asked Sensei anything about today. He didn't know the right answer to this question.

He could screw this up completely.

"Well, I..."

His voice was actually trembling slightly. He was scared. Scared of a little small talk.

Ugh. I haven't changed a bit.

"I read all sorts of stuff, I guess. Anything that catches my eye..." It was the vaguest, most harmless answer that he could think of.

"I see," Ruri responded. It was a noncommittal, nothing response, and the conversation ground to a halt.

Naomi *hated* himself in that moment.

This wasn't right at all.

What kind of conversation was *that*? It wasn't the way classmates should talk to each other, or friends. It *definitely* wasn't a conversation between a soon-to-be boyfriend and girlfriend.

A gust of wind blew by, and the small flowers on the riverbank swayed back and forth. The sun glittered on the river. Cars passed in the distance.

All of it just seemed to emphasize the awkward silence.

He needed to say *something*. If this kept up much longer, she was going to decide he was a fundamentally boring person. Or maybe just a jerk.

But Naomi's mouth didn't want to move. He couldn't force out a single syllable. He felt about ready to cry.

"I'm a fan of adventure novels, personally."

The silence was broken. Startled, Naomi looked up from the ground; Ruri was gazing out at the river as it flowed peacefully by.

"The heroes of those books throw themselves into their journeys. They face terrible challenges, but they never give up. That's always appealed to me." She was looking up, now, to where the moon hung palely in the sky. "I want to live my life that way, too," she continued. "That's the kind of person I want to be."

Ruri had opened up to him; she'd just told him something *real* about herself. She'd taken the risk of exposing her actual thoughts and feelings. Naomi felt like she'd just given him a big push forward. He *had* to meet her halfway here. He owed her that much.

It wouldn't be fair to let one person drag the cart along all by herself.

"So, actually..." His voice still trembled, unfortunately. "I like science fiction."

He could tell she'd turned to look at him, but he couldn't look at her himself. Instead of meeting her gaze, he focused on getting the words out coherently.

"Those books show you whole new worlds, right? And they're really amazing, bizarre worlds, totally different from our own. But they're not just made up out of nothing. You've got the *science* part there, too, to tie them to reality."

The words flew out of him like an avalanche now. He was talking too fast, almost babbling. If he'd seen someone else speaking like this, he would have felt embarrassed on their behalf. But he just couldn't stop.

"Those worlds are fiction, of course, but they feel like an *extension* of the one we really live in. So it kind of feels like our world's part of the story. It makes me feel like I'm a character in a story, too." His slowing down and losing its confidence—he hadn't planned this out in advance, so he was seriously startling to ramble. "I mean, I know I'm just a minor character, but...well... I guess I can't explain it very clearly." He pushed through it with sheer willpower, like a marathon runner closing in on the finish line. "But anyway, I love science fiction."

He'd said everything he could.

Ruri responded "I see" for the second time—another blank reply.

Naomi felt the anxiety he'd suppressed bubbling back up again. He'd taken a real gamble here. He'd rolled the dice, but there was no telling what the outcome might be. He'd told her about himself, about what he really thought and felt. Instead of reading off some line from a notebook, he'd given her *his* words, just as they'd popped into his head.

What if she thought they were ridiculous?

What if she disagreed with him completely?

It would almost be too much to—

"I think..."

Naomi looked over to find she was looking back at him.

"I know what you mean."

Naomi couldn't describe what he felt in that moment very well. Putting it into words would have cheapened the feeling somehow, or even destroyed it. But there was one thing he could say for sure.

It was the happiest he'd ever been in his sixteen years of life.

As they prepared to resume their trek, one book on the cart caught Naomi's attention.

It was a novel with a striking cover, although it looked like an older book. Its corners were rounded and worn, and there was a big stain on it, too.

He picked it up and examined it. The illustration on the cover suggested that a huge, complex world awaited him inside. His curiosity was piqued.

"I think I might want to read this one."

"You're welcome to take it, if you want."

It was a nice offer, and it made him happy. But this was a book she was donating to the sale, and it hadn't been put on sale just yet.

"I'll just have to buy it once the sale starts, I think."

Hopefully it won't be too expensive.

Wondering how they would set the prices, Naomi flipped through the book idly...and found something unexpected at the very back.

"Oh, look. It's an old library book." On the inside of the back cover, there was a paper pocket with a yellowed card inside. These cards had been part of the Kyoto Library's lending system at some point in the past; you wouldn't find them in any books in active circulation now. Sometimes you'd spot one in an old used book, though.

"He must have gotten it from a branch that was trimming its collection," said Ruri, leaning over to take a look. She pulled out the card, with its list of dates in the past and handwritten names—more than ten entries in total.

When you borrowed this book, you wrote your name on the card, then the next borrower did the same. It had probably seemed normal in an era without computer databases, but...

"That's kind of nice, isn't it?" Naomi said vaguely.

Ruri nodded with a small smile. "The first person to check it out got to write their name at the very top. That must have felt really good."

Naomi nodded in agreement. Maybe any booklover would understand the appeal of those cards.

By the time they made it to the front gate of Nishiki High,

the sun was already setting. Breathing heavily, Naomi slowly lowered the handcart's front bar. His legs quivered with fatigue.

He double-checked the time just to be sure, but as expected, the trip had taken them over two hours. One trip today really was the most they could hope for, and it would likely be the same deal tomorrow. He might not even have the stamina for trips several days in a row.

For now, though, they needed to find a place to stash all these books. Lucky for them, a familiar group of people was just emerging from inside the school grounds.

"Ruru! Where did you get all of those?!" Kadenokouji Misuzu and a few other library committee members gathered around the handcart, wide-eyed with surprise.

Naomi found himself looking down at the ground. No one else had worried much about the book sale, but now they knew how seriously he and Ruri were taking it. It was honestly embarrassing. Working hard was nothing to be ashamed of, sure, but it took some courage to act so differently from everyone else.

Ruri didn't seem the slightest bit embarrassed, of course. She never did. She explained where the books came from without a hint of hesitation or shyness.

Misuzu flashed a big, brilliant smile and clapped her hands together.

The next afternoon, there were more than a dozen people crowded into the little storage building. A chain of teenagers passed along boxes and bags full of books bucket-brigade style.

A big, muscular third year carried huge boxes of oversized books all by himself.

Once they'd emptied the shelves, they all trekked back to school together. With the rusty old handcart in the lead, they formed a convoy of sorts, with carts and wheelbarrows they'd borrowed from the school following close behind.

With so many more people around to help, the handcart moved a lot faster than yesterday. A few of the boys took shifts on the handcart, including Naomi.

At one point, as he was shoving the thing along, Misuzu trotted up and whispered, "You went to Ruru's house, huh?" in a voice only he could hear. When he asked her what that was supposed to mean, she just smiled enigmatically at him like a goddess of love.

The group cleared out a space behind the school building, near the rear gate, and piled up their enormous haul.

They'd managed to move everything over in a single long afternoon. It had seemed like a hopeless job to do in three days, but they'd finished it entirely in one. That was the power of numbers.

"Think we should lug 'em all up to the library?"

"Seems like a waste of time. Why don't we get the teachers' permission to leave them out here for the next two days?"

As the chairman and older students talked it over, another upperclassman came trotting out with a flagpole and stand. The wrinkled flag had the words *Library Committee Used Book Sale* written on it.

"Oh wow, haven't seen that in a while."

"When was the last time we used it?"

Apparently the flag had been gathering dust for years. It didn't inspire any nostalgia in the first years, of course, but it did add a touch of festival atmosphere to everything.

"Ruru!" called Misuzu, trotting over with her arms outstretched.

"Stop calling me that, please," Ruri replied automatically for what had to be the thousandth time.

"This is amazing! I feel a little bad, though—you donated an entire library, and we barely chipped in at all!"

"It's fine. They were just lying around gathering dust, anyway. They'll be happier if they end up with someone who wants to read them."

"Aw, Ruru..."

"Cut it out."

It was genuinely hard to tell if the two girls liked each other or not. But while Ruri did look a bit annoyed about her nickname, she didn't seem to mind the conversation itself. People who didn't know them would have assumed they were friends, and Naomi was inclined to agree.

Ruri could probably get by fine all on her own, but maybe she didn't have to. Maybe this miniature festival would help her open up to the others, at least a little.

A group of three girls had now formed around Ruri, chatting cheerfully.

Naomi felt as happy as if he'd made a new friend himself.

9.

THE DISASTER THAT FOLLOWED was pure bad luck. They'd piled up the books by the rear gate, where neither students nor teachers went very often. They'd left that flagpole in its stand. Nobody had seen a reason why that might be a problem. They'd covered up the books that weren't in boxes with sheets of newspaper, to protect them in case it started raining. And the rear gate had a newly installed, motion-activated security light. The teacher who'd given them permission to leave the books back there didn't know about it either.

That night, the wind picked up.

The flag blew over, covering up the light, which turned it on automatically. Soon, the fabric started to smoke.

By the time the students arrived at school the next morning, the area near the back gate was fenced off by yellow tape. Police officers had been ducking under that tape for some time as they came and went from the scene. Inside this restricted area, there was another, smaller taped-off space; within it was a huge lump of smoking ashes. The only things that hadn't burned away completely were a few pieces of melted plastic and the charred remnants of some thicker old covers.

The fire had started in the middle of the night. Fortunately, the residents nearby had noticed it quickly, and the fire department had put out the blaze before it could spread to the school building. The only damage had been to the library committee's belongings out in back.

In the morning, the police had arrived to examine the scene. This was a huge event for a high school, of course, so a crowd of onlookers watched from a distance.

"A fire?"

"Wow, looks like it was going for a while."

"I'm just glad it didn't burn down the building, too..."

While most of the spectators whispered excitedly to each other, there was one group of onlookers who didn't say a word—the members of the library committee, the people who'd spent their afternoon bringing those books here, just watched in stunned silence.

Misuzu and Ruri were part of that group. Ruri's eyes were still and cold, like lumps of burnt-out charcoal that would never catch fire again. She was staring at a small piece of a book cover, one of the few scraps that survived the blaze.

It was a chunk of that beat-up old novel Naomi had wanted to buy.

From the rooftop, the sky was an unbroken field of blue. The city, and the mountains that surrounded it, looked the same as ever.

The world kept on turning, no matter what happened.

"If you knew it would happen..." Naomi's voice shook slightly, different from the way it had trembled the other day on the riverbank. "Couldn't we have prevented this?"

"That would have thrown history off track," Sensei replied flatly. "Our goal is to save her life. To make that happen, we need your relationship to develop as recorded. The fire was a necessary part of that process."

Naomi raised his hands reflexively. He wasn't sure if he wanted to grab Sensei by the collar, or just throw a punch at him. He'd never done either of those things before to *anyone*. But even as he reached out, he realized it was pointless. His hands slipped ineffectually through Sensei's body, quickly losing their momentum.

He couldn't do anything. He couldn't even vent his anger on this man in Ruri's stead. With no outlet to escape through, his anger swirled around in his head aimlessly, feeding on itself.

Memories of the days they'd spent preparing for the book sale flashed through his mind. How they'd gone around asking people to help them out, and that first sweaty trip back with that cart full of books. The way everyone had chipped in to help.

They'd worked so hard. All for nothing.

And Sensei had known all about it from the start.

"The used book sale was canceled." Naomi looked up. Sensei was staring down at him; he flinched slightly. There was strength in those eyes. This man had chosen his path, and he wouldn't be diverted from it. He was absolutely determined to reach his goal.

Naomi could understand that. He *was* Sensei, on some level—it made sense that he could follow the man's thought process.

Sensei was desperate.

Just as Naomi had thrown himself into gathering those books, Sensei had thrown himself into his plan. He knew the fire would be a sad, painful event, but he was convinced that it was *necessary*.

"The canceled sale depressed her deeply. I wanted her to cheer up, so I made a conscious effort to talk to her more often than before. It brought us closer."

Sensei paused for a moment, then issued his next order.

"You're going to do the same."

With those words, he strode past Naomi and disappeared. There would be no further explanations. He expected Naomi to simply do as he was told.

It was the *correct* answer, after all—according to his notebook.

10.

NAOMI WATCHED his desk clock closely. It was a digital model with large numbers and read 11:58.

He didn't want to leave too early or too late. He'd decided to wear a sweatsuit for this, as he felt it might involve some exercise. He had a backpack on too, but it was empty. He couldn't decide what to pack.

As midnight ticked closer, Naomi looked down at his hands. He wore the God Hand on his right. That had been his biggest worry at first, but fortunately, the crow transformed itself into the glove without complaint, just like it did during his morning training sessions.

As the display silently switched to 12:00, Naomi stepped quietly out of his room.

He took care to leave the apartment as quietly as possible. Their old, heavy front door tended to squeak at the slightest provocation, so he closed it carefully and locked it behind him.

When he turned around, he found Sensei standing in the hallway in front of him.

"Where do you think you're going?"

Naomi froze up. A jolt of fear ran through him; he felt like a zebra staring down a lion. Swallowing, he clutched the wrist of his gloved hand.

"I'm going to use the God Hand," he squeaked out, "to recreate those books."

"Don't be an idiot!"

Sensei strode up to Naomi and glared down at him.

"I *did* explain how that thing works, didn't I? Information-dense objects are exponentially harder to create or modify. And a single book is *packed* full of information. Are you planning to copy out every single page, word by word? Do you know how many hours that would take?"

It was a barrage of words. He wasn't yelling, but there was a clear, cold anger in his tone.

"Even if you somehow succeeded, you'd be altering the course of history. If the used book sale *isn't* canceled, my manual won't be useful anymore. You won't end up dating her. And we'll have no way to predict how the accident might play out."

Naomi flinched again. Sensei's words were hitting home.

"If we can't save her, it would be *your* fault."

It was true, of course. Everything he was saying was the

truth. Sensei knew the correct choice. He had the right answers. Saving Ruri's life was far more important than a used book sale.

Which meant—

"The reason..."

"What was that?"

Naomi was going to be wrong.

"The reason we're preventing this accident...is so Ichigyou-san can be happy." He stared back into Sensei's eyes with the fiercest expression he could muster. "But right now, she's miserable."

There wasn't any rational logic behind this choice. Naomi knew he was letting his emotions take over. This wasn't the safe path; it led directly into the unknown.

To the best of his ability, Naomi avoided taking risks. He didn't like challenging himself unless the outcome was predictable. His mind screamed at him to stop.

But he was still going to make the wrong choice. He was heading down the path of risk and uncertainty, where failure was more likely than success.

Sensei wanted him to stop. Stopping was clearly the smarter decision.

So what?

He wasn't doing this for Sensei, or for himself. He was doing it for *her.*

He walked past Sensei, picking up the pace with every step. Sensei couldn't touch him or stop him. He was grateful for that now.

Without looking back, he ran down the dark, deserted street toward the high school.

Deep inside the darkened library, Naomi flipped on a single desk lamp. He wasn't about to turn on the overhead lights and risk a security guard discovering him.

Some careful sneaking had brought him undetected to the second floor of the library. He didn't have a key, of course, but he'd used his glove to open a convenient hole in the entrance door.

The hole-opening part wasn't too difficult, but he'd struggled a little bit with repairing the door afterward. He'd always thought of the school doors as nothing but planks of wood, but they were actually composite objects with layers of veneer and protective coating; he couldn't recreate all that instantly. It would have been easier to make his hole in the glass part of the door, in retrospect.

Naomi checked his watch; it was 12:30 a.m. By 6:30 or so, the teachers and students with early morning activities would start trickling in. He needed to make as many books as possible in that time.

Crouching down next to his lamp, Naomi held his right hand out a few inches above the floor.

The first ninety minutes slipped by before he knew it.

Naomi focused on his task intently. His glove vibrated. And in the space under his palm, a book materialized out of thin air. This was his third creation so far. The first and second were nowhere to be seen, however. He'd erased both of them shortly after creating them.

The book had taken form quite nicely this time. Naomi remembered it clearly as one of the volumes he'd seen in Ruri's storage building. Although it was technically brand new, it looked appropriately worn and aged; a glance at the side showed that the paper was visibly yellowed.

The moment he picked it up and opened it, though, Naomi grimaced. Its contents were pure gibberish.

There were letters on the pages, aligned in neat sentences and paragraphs, resembling a novel in their length and spacing. But there wasn't a single coherent phrase to be found in any of it. It was the kind of nonsense you'd see when a computer screwed up encoding a text file. There were even a few bizarre symbols mixed in with the real characters. This wasn't something you could *read.*

His first and second tries had the exact same problem. Naomi understood why he'd failed. He'd been practicing with the God Hand for two and a half months by now, after all. He had a good sense for the way it worked in practice.

It could only create things he could *imagine.* There was no way he could use it to recreate the text of a book he'd never read.

Sensei had asked him if he planned to copy out the books *word by word.* That was clearly the only real way it could be done. He'd need to flip through a book while creating a copy of it.

But the original books had been destroyed. They were only

ashes at this point, and even those had been dumped in the trash by now.

Sensei knew all of this. He'd warned Naomi in advance that this project simply wasn't possible. If he really wanted to, he probably could have taken the glove back somehow, but he hadn't bothered. Maybe he'd decided to let Naomi frustrate himself instead.

Maybe he knew Naomi would come back beaten and defeated.

A dark, miserable feeling spread through Naomi's mind. He knew this sensation very well—he'd experienced it countless times. It was like an old friend by now.

Resignation.

Everything was telling him to give up, that there was nothing more to be done. There was no time. His goal was impossible. The glove couldn't do what he wanted it to.

He understood that all too well.

"So what?" he muttered defiantly to himself, picturing her face. "So what?!" It didn't matter if this was pointless. He just didn't want to give up. He *wouldn't.*

He felt his face distorting like a frustrated toddler's. He crumpled up the useless book in his hand.

He felt the glove quivering.

Blinking, he looked down at it. It really *was* quivering. He wasn't consciously trying to create anything at the moment; it was moving all on its own.

The part on the back of his hand began to shift and ripple. A long, thin cord emerged; at the end there was a bit that looked like a camera lens. It wriggled into place, then began emitting light—almost like a projector.

A holographic image took shape in front of him. His eyes went wide. This technology was *familiar*—he saw images of things like it nearly every morning at his training sessions, as a part of his daily lectures.

This thing was far more advanced than any technology in Naomi's world. There was only one person who could be using it.

"Sensei?"

There was no reply, but the blurry, vague image grew sharper, forming a clearly defined holographic model. He was looking at an old, stuffed bookshelf, one of the shelves from the old storage building.

Naomi reached out to the 3D model. As his hand drew closer, one of the books popped off the shelf and floated up in front of him.

He moved his hand experimentally; the holographic book responded, spinning in midair. After a moment, he managed to open it.

"Wait, is this..."

Closing the 3D model of the book, he reached out for another. It popped out just as easily.

Finally, he understood.

This was his source material—the guide he needed to reconstruct those burned books. Somehow, Sensei had provided him perfect reproductions of the books as they had been. This was the breakthrough he'd been hoping for. It was his chance to *succeed*.

Naomi looked up at the ceiling of the library—something told him Sensei was in that direction. "Thank you so much!" he whispered fiercely.

There was no reply, of course. But Naomi thought he could hear someone mutter, "What a moron," anyway. And then add, "Focus on the job at hand."

Naomi checked his watch. It was 1:35 a.m.

With this reference material, he could recreate the books perfectly. The only question now was how many he could finish before his time ran out. He had five hours—or *only* five hours, really. How far could he get?

Snapping the 3D book shut, he held his hand out once again. He didn't have any time to waste on thinking about it. He might not even get through ten books at this rate. Even five might be tough.

But despite the risks, he felt *joyful* as he threw himself into the task. A part of him was scared he might not succeed, but a bigger part of him was happy that he didn't have to give up yet.

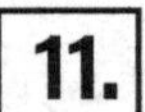

11.

NISHIKI HIGH STUDENTS flowed down Horigawa Street. It was a perfectly ordinary morning and a perfectly normal day—just another weekday in June. The Culture Festival and Sports Day were still far away, exams weren't for a while, and there weren't any special events scheduled.

Some of the students walking toward the front gate seemed happy or excited; others looked tired or annoyed. But none of them looked at all unusual.

Ruri was one of the students in the crowd, perfectly composed. There were no powerful emotions coursing through her; her mind was like the surface of a placid lake.

Yesterday, the library committee's books had all been burned to ashes.

Ruri had put a great deal of effort into gathering them up over the last three weeks. And most of them had belonged to her grandfather—books she had grown up admiring and reading. They were special to her. She was sad that they were gone, of course.

But that wasn't the main thing on her mind.

Yesterday, the committee chairman had sent a group message telling everyone that the used book sale was officially canceled. That knowledge cast a deep shadow over her thoughts.

She'd been looking forward to it.

It wasn't that she'd expected anything to come of it. There wasn't a concrete objective she'd been working toward. But as she devoted herself to gathering books, she'd started to think of the sale's success as a worthwhile goal in itself.

Ruri had always been uncomfortable in groups. In middle school, she'd kept her communication with her classmates to the bare minimum, mostly for assignments and the like. But after entering high school, she'd found herself on the library committee, working closely with a boy from her class. Then she'd started collaborating with the whole group, giving their project everything she had. That was all new for her.

It had been a kind of adventure.

She'd thrown herself at a new, totally unfamiliar challenge. She'd risked interacting with others. She'd grown closer to a stranger, and she'd overcome her fears. Maybe the average person wouldn't think she was doing anything unusual—those things came naturally to most people, it seemed. But for Ruri, it *had* been an adventure, one she'd wanted to face head on and triumph over, like the protagonists from her favorite stories.

But reality wasn't a children's book. Adventures don't always end in success and glory; sometimes, no matter how hard you try, you fail for no good reason. Her family's books had burned to ashes, and the used book sale wasn't even going to happen.

Ruri found herself remembering something her new friend Naomi had told her earlier in the week: "*I know I'm just a minor character.*"

She understood exactly what he meant.

Ruri didn't think of herself as a minor character in someone else's story, but she clearly wasn't a protagonist, either. She didn't have any magic ability to counteract this disaster, and no one was going to swoop in to fix things for her. No hero was coming. This was the real world, after all.

It was obvious, really. There was nothing worth whining about. The grown-ups of the world had learned these lessons long ago; they were just facts of life.

Ruri's heart was calm. It was calm *because* she understood, now, that she wasn't in a story.

She was just another ordinary person.

"Hey, Ichigyou-san..."

Someone called to Ruri at the shoe lockers by the entrance. She recognized the voice at once—she'd heard it a lot lately. Ruri turned to Naomi, but at the sight of his face, she couldn't suppress a small frown. It was first thing in the morning, but Naomi appeared completely exhausted. There were deep bags under his half-opened eyes, and his whole face drooped.

At first, she wondered if he'd pulled an all-nighter, but this level of fatigue suggested something else. He looked like he hadn't slept in days—but he'd seemed perfectly fine yesterday. There was something more to it.

Naomi offered Ruri a weak smile, then tottered off toward the library, beckoning her to follow.

There was a single cardboard box sitting on top of the checkout desk. At Naomi's urging, Ruri opened it uncertainly.

Her eyes went wide.

The box was full of old books. She knew some of them. She *recognized* some of them. There were forty or so, clearly books from her grandfather's collection. But that wasn't *possible*.

"Turns out there was one box that got stashed somewhere else. I found it yesterday," Naomi explained with a smile.

Still doubting her own eyes, Ruri picked up one of the books. As she held it in her hand, she finally believed it was real. It had the weathered feel of an old book; its pages were yellowed, and it even had a few familiar bumps and scrapes.

The still waters of her heart...rippled. Her chest felt oddly hot.

Some of them had survived. They hadn't all burned to ash. It lit a new fire in Ruri's heart.

If we have these, maybe...

"There's less than fifty in there," Naomi said, "but that's enough to hold a book sale, right?"

Her eyes still fixed on the box, Ruri nodded firmly.

They could do this. They'd lost almost all their stock, so it was back to being a small event, but that didn't matter. They could have the book sale after all.

She felt genuine joy bubbling up inside her.

That was when she noticed it. Her eyes settled on one particular book inside the box, familiar to her, like the others. She picked it up, a strange electric tingle running through her body.

It was an old novel with an attractive cover, but its corners were rounded and worn, and there was a big stain on it, too. It was the book Naomi had told her he was interested in, the one with the library card mounted on the inside of the back cover.

It had burned to ashes yesterday.

Ruri's thoughts spun through her mind in a confused jumble. It didn't make any sense—this book had been destroyed. She'd seen a charred fragment of its cover. Had her eyes played tricks on her? How could it be here if it had burned up in the fire?

Or had Naomi somehow found a different copy of this book last night? That didn't seem too realistic. There were more than forty books in this box; he couldn't possibly have bought them all in one night and made them look convincingly used. And he couldn't possibly have known about some of these familiar little dings. It would have required actual *magic*.

Uncertainly, she looked over in search of answers. She met his eyes.

Katagaki Naomi beamed at her.

"Thank goodness some of them were all right."

In that moment, Ruri understood, somehow. The truth of it jumped directly into her mind, bypassing conscious thought or logic.

It was him. He had done *something* to make this happen. She had no idea what; there was no plausible explanation. But there was no doubt in her mind.

Ruri opened her mouth to speak; she had so many questions. But before she could get a single word out, Naomi's head swung toward her. He pitched forward limply, his forehead hitting her shoulder.

Startled, Ruri just barely managed to grab hold of him and ease his fall to the ground.

She looked at his face. She'd never seen it this close before. Naomi was breathing softly and regularly in his sleep. His slack face suggested that he was utterly exhausted. What on earth had he been *doing* to wear himself out like this? Well, that was the one question she knew the answer to.

He'd been working magic.

He'd done it for the used book sale. For the group. Maybe

even for Ruri herself. He'd made it in the nick of time and saved her.

The hero had showed up after all.

"Eeeeek!" A shrill cry broke the silence. Ruri looked up to see Misuzu hopping excitedly in the library entrance.

"Ruru! Eee! Katagaki-kun! Hee hee hee!"

The meaning of her shrieks was unclear at best, but Ruri got the general idea. How was she going to explain any of this, exactly?

As Misuzu pranced into the room, the other library committee members began to trickle in behind her. It was odd; the message about the book sale being canceled went out yesterday, so there was no reason for them to be here instead of heading to their classrooms.

Finally, the committee's chairman walked in and looked around the library at the others.

"What, you too?"

He reached into his bag and retrieved a few books. The others took that as their cue to open their backpacks and tote bags to take out their own contributions. There were novels, how-to guides, even coffee-table books—their size and content varied widely. Before long, they'd formed a nice pile on the check-out counter.

At the very end, Kadenokouji Misuzu triumphantly added a romance novel with a cover full of hearts, placing it ceremoniously on the pile like the crown at a coronation.

Ruri smiled. Her little adventure wasn't quite over yet.

12.

NAOMI'S EYES slowly cracked open.

A thin curtain swayed in front of him. Through it, he could see the sky—a mix of blue and orange. It was either evening or dawn, but he had no idea which.

What time is it...?

If it was evening, the day was practically over. And if it was dawn, it was actually *tomorrow*. Either way, too much time had passed.

"Wait..." His eyes went wide. "The book sale!"

Naomi popped up to a sitting position, his heart pounding in his chest. Not good—he'd fallen asleep!

His mind finally managed to piece together where he was—in the side room in the library, lying on one of the couches. How many hours had he been here? Was the day already over? What had happened with the book sale?

"We couldn't wake you up," someone said.

Startled, Naomi turned toward the voice, and once again blinked in confusion. Ichigyou Ruri was sitting on the smaller sofa, looking as self-possessed as always with her usual calm expression on her face. But her *outfit*...that was another story.

She was wearing a frilly white apron over a bright blue dress. Her poofy skirt looked like it might flip up if she turned around too quickly, and he couldn't even look at her tights without blushing. He recognized the look—it was a classic "Alice in Wonderland" costume. That didn't help him make sense of the situation, though. Why was she *wearing* that?!

"I decided I'd sell as many books as possible," Ruri said after a moment. It sounded like this was her attempt at explaining herself, and her tone suggested it hadn't been an easy decision. Naomi had to assume that Misuzu had worn her down.

"Oh! Wait!" said Naomi, his mind finally jumping back to the most important topic. "Does that mean, uh...did the book sale...?" His voice trailed off hesitantly. All he could remember was handing over a single box of books to Ruri in the morning. He'd passed out immediately afterward. He had no idea how things had gone after that.

For all he knew, once the sale had been canceled, they hadn't been able to reverse that decision. The box might be sitting under the front counter right now. Naomi stared at Ruri with all the fear of a defendant waiting for his verdict.

In response, she reached into the pocket of her apron and took out a piece of paper. She unfolded it carefully, then held it out dramatically for Naomi's inspection.

Used Book Sale: SOLD OUT! Total Donations: 34,850 yen!

Naomi just stared at it blankly, then clenched his hands into fists. But just squeezing them tightly wasn't enough—he threw his arms up in triumph.

I did it.

Pure joy pulsed through his veins. All the pain and exhaustion he'd endured the previous night melted from his mind.

I pulled it off. I didn't give up for once, and it worked!

"Katagaki-san..." Naomi looked over at Ruri and started in

surprise. She'd moved to the chair right next to his sofa; she was staring at him from only a few feet away.

"Thank you." The words were simple, but her tone was heartfelt. Naomi could feel himself blushing. He understood, of course, that she was thanking him for finding that box of books. She had no idea that he'd spent all night *making* them with a magical glove. There wasn't anything special about her gratitude.

"Hey, no problem," he responded with a smile.

He'd assumed that would end the conversation, but for some reason, Ruri was still staring at him intently. She didn't seem to feel they were done yet.

"Uhm, it's not like I really did anything that—"

"Thank you very much," Ruri interrupted with a shake of her head.

Then, she smiled at him.

Naomi didn't have time to brace for impact. It took a few moments for him to even understand what he was feeling. The first symptom was purely physical; there was a wonderful warmth in his chest that showed no signs of fading. Finally, he managed to put words to it.

That smile was the most beautiful thing he'd seen in his entire life.

Melodramatic as it might sound, he knew he would never forget this moment. No matter what else happened, no matter how long he lived, he was going to treasure that smile forever.

"You know..." Naomi was a little surprised to hear his own voice. His mouth seemed like it was moving all on its own.

He wanted to say it. He really, truly did. His conscious mind was holding him back, though. Was there really a point to telling her now? Who knew what would happen? Everything might fall apart.

"I, uh..."

So what? Just say it. It's the truth.

"I love you, Ichigyou-san."

Naomi's gaze fell to the floor as he spoke. He couldn't bear to look at anything else in that moment—not at himself, and certainly not at her.

He'd said it.

He'd actually said it.

"I see," Ruri replied.

Maybe this was what it felt like when a judge sentenced you to death.

"Well, it takes two people to have a relationship."

Naomi's eyes widened in surprise. These weren't the words he'd been expecting to hear.

"I suppose..."

Slowly, cautiously, he looked up.

"We can give it a try together."

That same smile was waiting for him.

There was a book sitting on the table in that side room; it was the beat-up old novel that had caught Naomi's eye. Ruri had set it aside for him during the book sale.

The pocket inside its back cover still had that yellowed paper card sitting inside it. Scribbled across the neatly printed lines were the names of everyone who'd ever borrowed it, in order, starting from the top.

And on the very first line, in faded ink that was by now only barely legible, was the name *Ichigyou Ruri*.

CHAPTER FOUR

1.

WHEN NAOMI WAS YOUNG, he would sometimes look up at the moon and reach for it. He used to think he might just barely touch it if he stood on top of Kyoto Tower.

Back then, he hadn't known that the moon was 380,000 kilometers away from Earth, and since learning that fact, he'd never reached at it again. He wasn't a child anymore, after all.

But now, he found himself reliving that experience. It was a peculiar feeling.

"Now! *Imagine* as hard as you can!" shouted Sensei, his voice echoing across the forested hill. He needed to shout to make himself heard; their training ground, in a secluded part of the Narabigaoka forest, was currently a *very* noisy place. "Let your mind run wild!"

Naomi's glove vibrated fiercely. The roaring sound that filled the air was produced by the God Hand when it was operating under a heavy load. Fierce winds whipped around the area and lashed the trees back and forth; clods of soil were pulled out of the ground. The world groaned in protest as he *rewrote* it.

Naomi closed his hand, clutching at nothingness. His fingers wrapped around a small gray-white orb. He'd created it in a split second, simply by picturing it in his mind's eye.

He'd realized his childhood fantasy. He was holding the moon.

"More! Stretch yourself even further. You can do anything!" shouted Sensei.

Dropping the small sphere to the ground, Naomi immediately began his next creation.

Sensei was right. Naomi had caught the moon in his hands; surely they could stretch even further. The air swirled violently once more as he rewrote reality, defining mass and volume out of nothing. His knowledge fed his imagination and gave his mental image greater precision.

He shaped a complex mixture of heavy metals and silicon into a reddish-brown lump of rock. He had created Mars.

"Whatever you visualize can be made real. There's nothing, literally *nothing*, that can stop you."

Naomi tossed the small planet aside. Pulsing with excitement, driven on by Sensei's words, he reached out even further into the universe. Every time he created something new, he felt like his brain might break down under the strain. Still, he kept pushing further, testing the limits of his mind. He brought forth liquid iron and nickel and surrounded them with silicates. In the blink of an eye, in the palm of his hand, he reproduced a core, mantle, and crust that had taken eons to form in space. Venus.

"Tell yourself this world is *yours*. Tell yourself..."

Gritting his teeth, Naomi squeezed the last few drops of strength from his brain. This wasn't impossible. He wasn't at his limit. He could push past this—he *had* no limits.

Something new took shape in the palm of his right hand.

He gathered hydrogen, the simplest of all elements. He created it, concentrated it, and created even more.

The little object began to grow hotter and hotter, denser and denser. And Naomi just kept going.

Sensei shouted once again, "You're going to be its *god*!"

And then, there was light.

It was like seeing the beginning of the universe—not that he could compare it to the real thing. Finally letting himself relax, Naomi felt the blood begin to drain from his overheated, exhausted brain. Its job was done now. He'd finished his creations.

Vacantly, he looked down at his hand, at the blazing ball of heat resting in it. Its surface was a single great river of flame, flowing slowly in multiple directions; every now and then, a pillar of fire would burst from its surface.

It was a tiny sun.

He looked up and met Sensei's gaze. For once, the man wasn't scowling at him. In fact, he was smiling.

"Not bad," he said, offering Naomi a thumbs-up. "I'll give that a passing grade."

It was July 2nd, and this was their final training session. Naomi had passed his examination and become a god.

2.

[July 3rd—The Uji River Fireworks Festival]

THERE WERE TWO TRAIN STOPS in the Uji area: the Uji Station on Japan Railway's Nara line, and an identically named station on the Keihan Uji line. And today, both of them were absolutely packed with people.

The sun was nearly set; evening was giving way to night. The flow of people from across the city to the festival was reaching its peak. There were couples in yukatas, families with children in tow—people of all ages, in all kinds of different clothing, all heading in the same direction.

Some among the crowds were shooting uncertain glances up at the sky; the weather was the one point of concern at the moment. The area around the festival was covered in typical summer clouds, seemingly undecided whether they were going to rain on everyone's parade or not.

The people moved forward nonetheless, silently hoping for the best. But this time, Ichigyou Ruri wasn't among them.

"On July 3rd, we went to the Fireworks Festival together."

The voice seemed like it was coming directly into Naomi's ear. Reflexively, he reached up and touched the frame of the glasses he was wearing, which apparently had a small speaker built into them. Sensei was actually standing on top of a nearby utility pole.

The two of them waited just outside Ichigyou Ruri's house

in Shimogamo. Sensei was using his perch to keep an eye on her second-floor window.

"The weather took a sudden turn for the worse in the middle of the fireworks, and it turned into a thunderstorm. The exact time of the event itself was 8:01 p.m."

"Right. I didn't invite her this time, though."

Naomi could keep up his end of the conversation without shouting, fortunately; the glasses must've had a built-in microphone, too. This was Naomi's first time wearing the things, which he'd made with the God Hand to Sensei's precise instructions. In all honesty, he didn't quite understand how they worked. Making any sort of electronic gizmo was an extreme challenge for Naomi working on his own. But these glasses were connected to the God Hand by a cord, and the crow was apparently handling a lot of the more complex functions through that connection. He hadn't had to implement a lot of the technology himself.

Trying to ignore the unfamiliar weight on the bridge of his nose, Naomi looked up at the darkening sky. There were a few clouds visible, but it didn't look likely to rain.

"There won't be any thunder in this area, right? Doesn't this mean we've prevented the accident?"

"Assuming nothing happens before then, yes," Sensei said ominously.

"I can't imagine what *could* happen, though..."

But just as those words left Naomi's mouth, he spotted something at the very edge of his vision. There was someone standing in the middle of the residential road not too far away.

At first, he thought the figure was a construction worker, mainly because it was wearing a bright yellow belt that looked like a reflective vest. On closer examination, though, there was something very odd about it. Naomi had never seen a construction worker wearing a *kitsune* mask before.

It was a stylized, painted fox mask, the kind of thing you could find for sale at the gift shops around the Fushimi Inari shrine. But this was Shimogamo, not Inari, and the festival wasn't anywhere near this area. The person didn't look like a parade performer, anyway.

Naomi lowered his glasses, trying to get a better look at the strange figure. But as soon as he did, the man disappeared entirely.

"Huh?"

When he put the glasses back on, the man was still standing there, exactly where he'd been a moment before. And he was beginning to trudge in Naomi's direction.

He was invisible, except through the glasses. What did *that* mean?

"Damn it. They're here," growled Sensei.

"Wh-what is that thing?"

"It's the Homeostatic System," Sensei replied. The masked figure drew steadily closer as he spoke; Naomi couldn't help but take a step back from that seriously creepy thing. "It detected an alteration to AllTale's system files, and it's here to protect their integrity. Those things will try to erase any discrepancies in the records, returning the simulation to its predetermined state."

Those things, plural?

Naomi scanned the area, his heart thumping in his chest. Between one glance and the next, several identical masked figures materialized in the street around him. He quickly counted ten; more popped into existence by the second.

"In other words..." Naomi glanced up anxiously and met Sensei's gaze. "They're planning to drag you and your girlfriend to the Uji River, where you're *supposed* to be."

"What?! What should I do?!"

"Fight them, obviously."

"You want me to *fight* a computer system? How?"

"Use the God Hand, idiot. Make yourself a weapon!"

Unsettled as he was, Naomi instantly crouched down and pressed his glove to the ground. He didn't see weapons on a regular basis, unfortunately; they weren't exactly necessary for a high schooler in modern Japan. It was hard for him to even picture one on the spur of the moment.

"Whatever you make, the God Hand will enhance its performance. Just focus on visualizing something powerful!"

Powerful? Powerful how? Uh...okay. Something you could hurt somebody with. Something you could swing at someone's face. Something heavy. Something tough...

The glove trembled in response to Naomi's thoughts. He wasn't feeling too confident about the results this time, but in the next moment, there *was* something nice and thick and heavy in his hand.

He'd produced an encyclopedia.

Naomi was confused by this, even though it was entirely his own doing. You could certainly do some damage with a book if you swung it hard enough. But did it really qualify as a weapon?

He didn't have time to think the matter over. The masked things were only a few paces away. Rising to his feet, Naomi brandished the hefty book; a second glance revealed that it had a cord attached to it, like some kind of throwing weapon.

He grabbed hold of that seriously oversized bookmark with both hands and swung the book into the air like a shotput hammer.

"Argh!"

The encyclopedia smashed directly into the face of the nearest masked thing. The figure flew backward with astonishing force, bounced off the ground, and kept flying. A split second later, its body froze in midair with a strange, staticky sound, and that was where it stayed, totally immobilized.

Wow. That was easier than I thought.

"Nice," said Sensei, offering him a thumbs-up.

Pulling back his encyclopedia with a tug on the cord, Naomi saw a small flash of electricity as it zipped into his hands. Maybe this was the "performance enhancement" Sensei had mentioned.

One way or another, he had the ability to take these things out—to interfere directly with creatures that weren't even part of his world.

Maybe he could do this after all.

"Naomi."

The voice didn't come through his glasses this time. Sensei

had hopped down off the pole at some point; he was standing back-to-back with Naomi.

"You need to hold these things off until the time of the accident has passed. That's how you keep her safe. Just hold out another thirteen minutes!"

"What happens after that?"

"We'll cross that bridge when we come to it. Get moving!"

Naomi readied his weapon with a forceful nod—this wasn't the time for lengthy explanations. The street was already full of masked enemies.

Clearing his mind as best he could, he swung his encyclopedia-hammer at the nearest group. Several masked figures were sent soaring into the sky, where they froze. The things were still very creepy, but that was probably for the best. It made it easier to hit them without hesitation.

"They're moving inside! Get in the yard!" shouted Sensei from above. He'd returned to his perch on top of the utility pole.

The fox-masked things had breached the wall around the property and were making their way toward Ruri's house. Naomi rushed to follow, clambering into the yard; he'd briefly considered opening a hole in the wall instead but decided it would take too long to close it behind him.

By the time he made it over, there were already dozens of the things in the yard. Most of them must have appeared in there.

"Get lost!" Naomi arced his encyclopedia into the crowd, sending the masked things flying. With every blow, a few more froze awkwardly in midair. But he couldn't make a dent in their numbers; they spawned quicker than he could hit them. This wasn't looking good at all.

With a few more swings of his weapon, Naomi cut himself a path forward. He was managing, just barely, to keep the things away from Ruri's house.

Faster. Faster!

He pushed himself to attack more quickly, more viciously. But his desperation backfired; he tried to press forward decisively but took an awkward step and lost his balance. He pitched forward and tumbled to the ground.

Naomi pushed himself up out of the dirt. It was too late; a solid wall of the eerie fox-masks encircled him completely.

Rather than attacking, however, the things joined hands. A bluish-white electric light began to arc around the circle they'd formed around him.

"They're on the second floor!" shouted Sensei, his voice increasingly desperate.

Looking up, Naomi saw the same bluish light flashing through the window of Ruri's room. Electric sparks arced into the air just outside it.

Oh crap, that can't be good.

At the same moment that thought crossed his mind, he heard a loud *bzzzt*.

"Huh?" Stunned, Naomi looked around. The army of fox-mask men was gone, and the dirt under his feet was now a neatly paved stone path. He saw red handrails to both sides and could hear the sound of running water; he was on a bridge.

He could hear large crowds on both sides of the river.

"What the..." someone murmured behind him.

Startled, Naomi turned around to see Ichigyou Ruri lying on the ground, looking just as astonished as he felt. Her casual, baggy outfit suggested she'd been lounging in her bedroom only a moment earlier.

Those masked things had done something to her. To both of them.

Oh no. Oh crap. Is this bridge—

"Naomi!" Sensei's voice boomed out of Naomi's glasses. They must've still been in communication range, but when Naomi looked for him, the older man was nowhere in sight.

"Sensei! Where are we?!"

"The bastards just abused their system privileges," Sensei replied angrily. "They *moved* you right to the scene! You're right where the lightning strike is going to happen!"

It was just as he'd feared. They were stuck in the one place they really didn't want to be.

"Ichigyou-san!" Naomi hurriedly reached down and grabbed Ruri by the hand. They needed to run, right now. It didn't matter where.

But just as he was pulling her up, something else pulled her sharply *down*.

"Ow!"

Instead of rising to her feet, Ruri pitched forward and hit the ground, caught by the ankle. Naomi came closer and saw what had snagged her—it was the ground itself. The stone surface of the bridge had warped and coiled itself around her leg, chaining her solidly in place. It was the sort of trick Naomi usually pulled with the God Hand.

This was what *system privileges* really meant: the power to control and reshape the world around him.

His glove vibrating fiercely, Naomi ripped the stone apart. But the bridge reacted immediately, reforming the chain in the blink of an eye. This wasn't going to work; the system was too fast for him.

Springing to his feet, Naomi looked wildly from one side of the bridge to the other. There were thick crowds on either end. After a moment, he realized they weren't made up of humans—it was the army of fox-masks who had brought him here.

Their menacing silence conveyed their message clearly enough.

Stop trying to run. Stay right where you are. Let events continue the way they're supposed to.

Naomi looked up at the sky. The dark, stormy clouds above had started to rumble ominously.

"Two minutes left!" came the voice in his ear, tense and abrupt.

"Sensei..." Naomi called to future self, his voice pleading. He called to the man who'd trained him, who'd spent the last three months with him, guiding him and teasing him like a brother.

The days they'd spent in training flashed through his mind in rapid succession. From the day they'd met, they'd walked this road together.

"Listen, Naomi." His answer came, as always, not even a hint of despair in his tone. "This is it. This is the moment of truth.

Don't worry about the repercussions, all right?" Sensei paused for just a moment to let his instructions sink in, then went on. "Give those bastards a *real* show."

Naomi nodded in reply. His mind was already kicking into gear, visualizing what *a real show* might be. If he could visualize it, he could make it real.

Naomi held his right hand up toward the sky. Then, he began to focus.

A small sphere formed in the palm of his glove. It grew quickly to the size of a baseball, then to the size of a soccer ball, then even larger than Naomi himself.

The sphere writhed with motion, in a state of constant change. For a moment, its surface looked like iron. In the next, it was water, and then fire. It was everything at once, *everything* that made up this world, consolidated into a single ball of chaos.

"Nngh..." A grunt forced its way out of Naomi's mouth. His brain struggled under the strain, and blood coursed through his head like boiling water. Keeping himself conscious and focused took sheer willpower.

The sphere grew to the size of an oil storage tank.

From far away, Naomi could hear the crowds of spectators babbling in confusion. The sphere was visible to everyone on the banks of the river by now.

Sensei had told him to give them *a real show*, so he'd make this the evening's grand finale.

A flash of light tore through the sky, and thunder crashed. The moment of truth was finally here.

Naomi began to close his hand, trying to *grip* the enormous thing he'd created. Its sheer, impossible mass resisted fiercely, but little by little, his fingers squeezed around it, crushing it. The thing was practically a *planet*, but he was going to squeeze it down until it fit in his hand.

Is this really possible?

For a moment, Naomi's conviction wavered as the sheer implausibility of what he was doing overcame his powers of imagination. He wasn't anyone special, after all. He was just another nobody. Could he really pull off a miracle?

He faltered, knowing he was just one step before the goal line. His self-doubt, his indecisiveness, bogged him down, and he knew he was going to fail—

"I know you, Naomi," he heard, the words shoving him forward—words that, in a way, came from Naomi himself. "You can do this."

With all his strength, Naomi squeezed his hand shut. The enormous sphere he'd created pulsed inside his fist.

Then, he gently, carefully opened his hand again.

A small black sphere, about one centimeter in diameter, rose up into the air; although it seemed tiny and unobtrusive, the world distorted and twisted around it. Naomi tried to reduce its power with the glove, but it was too powerful to completely contain.

This wasn't something a human being was meant to control—the all-consuming remnant of a star, a black hole.

The sky flashed with blinding light and an ear-splitting roar shook the air. A great electric current hurtled down from the heavens at near-light speed, heading straight for Ichigyou Ruri, exactly as it was *meant* to.

But that bolt of lightning never hit her.

The black hole distorted its path. A torrent of energy coursed violently through the atmosphere; oxygen and water spun around the bridge with the force of a tornado.

Naomi pushed his imagination just a little further. He forced the world to change. And through his glasses, he saw the last remnants of the thunderbolt disappear into the abyss.

A thick fog had settled all around the bridge, probably from the river evaporating around it. As he stared blearily out at it, an idle thought slipped through Naomi's mind: *It kinda reminds me of a rock concert.*

It was oddly quiet. At first he thought he might have blown out his ears, but then he heard the faint sound of the river and realized his hearing was just fine.

Bit by bit, the fog began to clear, revealing his surroundings. He could make out the bridge railings, and the stone pavement, and...

And her. Sitting on the bridge with her mouth hanging open and her eyes wide.

She was alive. Ichigyou Ruri had survived.

"Katagaki-san?" she murmured in a small, stunned voice. Naomi stumbled forward, overwhelmed, and dropped to his knees in front of her. He needed to make sure it was real, that *she* was real, so he wrapped his arms around her.

She's really here. She's breathing, and I can feel her pulse.

She's alive.

"Ichigyou-san..." His voice cracked, something caught in his throat that mangled his voice, but he couldn't stop the words flowing out of him, either.

"You're...all right. I d-did it! I actually did it..."

He clung to her, sobbing, with tears rolling down his face. Yet again, he'd found a way to make himself an embarrassment. But then Ruri hugged him back, and he felt a little less ashamed.

Just then, he finally remembered about Sensei. He needed to share the good news right away—this was why Sensei had come from the future, after all.

With that thought, he finally regained his composure, and realized he'd been hugging Ruri for an awkwardly long time. Suddenly embarrassed, he pulled back and reached up to touch the side of his glasses, hoping they weren't broken.

"Sensei!"

The moment he called out to his mentor, Naomi realized he was already here, standing on one of the posts of the guardrail. When had he arrived?

"Sensei," he called out again, rising to his feet.

Ruri would probably find this a little odd, since the man was invisible to her. But he could explain everything to her later. Right now, he wanted nothing more than to celebrate this victory with his future self. He wanted to see Sensei's face glowing with joy.

For some reason, though, the man had his hood on again.

Most of his face was hidden in shadow. After a moment, he began to speak.

"The contents need to fit their vessel perfectly."

Naomi blinked in confusion.

"I had to eliminate the discrepancies between her digitized consciousness and the physical structure of her brain. I needed to get her mind as close as possible to the way it was at the very moment of the accident."

What is he talking about? I don't get it.

"The compatibility ratio finally broke the necessary threshold. As of this moment—"

"Um, Sensei—"

"I can *synchronize* her."

"What are you talking about?"

Sensei snapped his fingers.

Instantly, black wings sprouted from the glove on Naomi's right hand. They beat fiercely in the air, pulling it free; a moment later, it transformed back into the three-legged crow and flew off into the night sky.

Just as quickly, eight enormous *claws* rained down from the sky. Each the size of a pillar, they slammed into the stone surface of the bridge, forming a perfect octagon.

Ichigyou Ruri was in its center.

"The girl's in love," Sensei murmured. The space between the pillars solidified into glass-like walls. Ruri was trapped inside, like a fish in an aquarium. Naomi could see her shouting, but he couldn't hear anything.

"She fell head over heels for you, and that's what pushed her over the line. Her mental state is virtually identical to the way it was at the moment of that accident. Everything's *finally* ready."

I don't get it. What is he talking about? Isn't he supposed to be me? Why can't I understand him?!

Suddenly, the claw-like pillars grew taller. The octagonal aquarium stretched up into the starry sky and *pierced* it like a knife, opening a yawning hole.

"When that bolt of lightning hit her, she didn't actually die," Sensei said. "But she *was* left brain dead."

The inside of the tank filled up with light. The walls grew white. And Ruri, still shouting silently inside it, faded away into the brilliance.

Before she disappeared completely, Naomi thought he saw her call his name.

The claws jerked up out of the bridge. As if gravity had been reversed, the great cage *fell* up into the sky. And just like that, they disappeared, taking her with them.

Naomi and Sensei were left behind.

Naomi stared at his future self, disbelieving, his mind a blank. Then, and only then, did Sensei pull back his hood.

He was smiling. He looked genuinely happy.

"Thanks for everything, Naomi," he said. "And goodbye." With those words, he dissolved into tiny sparkles, almost like a little firework. Just like a firework, the sparkles quickly faded away into the night. Where he'd stood, there was only the darkness of the sky.

Naomi's fingers twitched involuntarily as he stared at the space where the light had been.

The night was hot and sticky. He could feel the humid, sauna-like air pressing directly against his bare, gloveless hands.

The fireworks were over for this year, another festival come to an end. But instead of trudging home, Naomi looked up at the silent sky and spoke in a soft, trembling voice.

"Sensei?"

HELLO WORLD
THE NOVEL

CHAPTER FIVE

1.

NAOMI OPENED HIS EYES. Without rising from his chair, he lifted his head up to look around. Morning light leaked into the room between the blinds.

The sounds of the hospital room were the same as always. The air conditioner hummed faintly, and the medical equipment array let out quiet beeps, the noise indicating that she was still alive.

Unfolding his arms, Naomi pressed his fingers to his temples. He'd pulled an all-nighter. Sleep had seemed completely impossible.

Twelve hours had passed since it happened.

Everything had gone according to plan. Sure, a few unexpected developments had popped up, but he'd accomplished his main goal perfectly.

It would be *fine.* Of *course* this would work...wouldn't it?

Logic and emotion fought for dominance in his mind. Any plan, no matter how carefully plotted and carried out, could end badly. There was no such thing as a guaranteed outcome, or so the cold, analytical scientist in him said.

The other part of him—the desperate, emotional part—just shouted "*it's going to be fine*" over and over again, an argument based mostly on wishful thinking.

It was a pointless conflict; he could bash his feelings against his rational mind all day long, and it wouldn't make the slightest difference. All he could do was wait.

But if this doesn't work...I don't know what I'll do...

An unfamiliar sound drew Naomi's attention over to the medical machinery. This was a new sound—one he was *sure* he'd never heard in the ten years he'd been visiting this room.

Beep.

He stared at the monitor on the largest machine, at the long, flat line it always displayed.

It had just *moved.*

Naomi sprang out of his chair. His knees buckled under him as he rose, pitching him forward; he grabbed the rail on the side of the bed and pushed himself back up.

The woman sleeping in that bed had an oxygen mask strapped to her face. She'd been hospitalized for a very long time, and the effects of that stay were painfully visible; she was emaciated, with hollow cheeks and an unnaturally thin neck and shoulders. But her chest still moved quietly under her thin blanket.

Leaning over the bed, Naomi stared down at the woman's face. The unfamiliar beeping of the machinery kept going.

It was the sound of *life*. Of brain activity.

The sound of a soul returned to its body.

He thought he could see her eyelids stirring just slightly. He watched intently as they slowly began to open. She flinched slightly as the light hit them for the first time in years.

Her pupils moved, first in one direction, then another.

She was looking at him. She was looking *right at him*, meeting his eyes with understanding in her own. She could see him. She knew he was there.

She was *conscious*.

"Oh God..."

Naomi heard himself speaking from what felt like a great distance. An overwhelming flood of feeling surged through him, moving his body against his will. He felt his face scrunching up and the tears running freely down his cheeks.

Collapsing forward, he wrapped his arms around the woman's slender body.

"I missed you, Ruri," he moaned, the words barely coherent. "I missed you so much!"

Her mouth moved slightly in response. But after all the time she'd spent asleep, her vocal cords couldn't make a sound.

Summer, 2037. At Kyoto Chubu General Hospital, Ichigyou Ruri awoke for the first time in a decade.

2.

THE TIP OF A CANE tapped at a regular rhythm against the polished floor of the hallway.

Katagaki Naomi made his way past the front desk and left Chubu General Hospital. The world outside was bright and sunny, the hot summer day cut by a breeze for once that improved things considerably.

He'd honestly wanted to stay at Ruri's bedside, but there wouldn't be much that he could do for her until later. It was going to take a long time for her to recover from the physical effects of a ten-year slumber, and he had to leave her rehab in the hands of the doctors and nurses. He wasn't a medical professional.

It might take a while, but in the full scope of things, it was nothing. She'd woken up. That was what *really* mattered.

Kamanza Street, a leafy avenue that ran past the front of the hospital, seemed more vibrantly green than usual today. Naomi turned down it, heading toward his work. He still had a few important things to do.

He led with his cane with each step, moving it cleanly and confidently with his right hand and forearm. Back when he'd first started using the thing, he'd struggled to walk even short distances with it. He'd never known that you used a cane with your right arm when your left leg was disabled, and getting the hang of it had been a challenge. He'd come to resent any building without a proper elevator.

But time and practice had gradually eliminated those problems. Now, he could move around as quickly as an able-bodied person.

As he waited for the light to change at the crosswalk, his phone started to buzz. Just as he'd anticipated, his job was calling.

He sent a quick *I'm on my way* and picked up his pace as he crossed the street.

The numbers on the elevator's screen ticked upward, the *B* next to them indicating that the car was plunging deep underground.

On the wall next to the buttons, an information panel listed every department and their floors. The names were technical, even indecipherable to a layman; one glance at the list would tell you this was a *staff-only* elevator. At the very top, in slightly larger font, were the words "Chronicle Kyoto Project Center."

The doors slid open onto a short hallway ending at an oddly bulky metal door. Naomi stepped out of the elevator and strode through the door. A camera installed in the wall above automatically scanned the faces of anyone who approached and identified whether they were authorized personnel. A second after it spotted Naomi, the door slid open automatically.

Instantly, the sound of panicked voices reached him.

"The unrecognized region is still expanding!" someone yelled. An array of green-tinted overhead lights illuminated the space; in a sunken, octagonal central area, researchers in uniform ran back and forth among numerous computer consoles, their movements frantic. At its very center, a cluster of anxious people had gathered around an enormous table monitor.

This was the AllTale Control Center.

His cane clacking against the tile floor, Naomi stepped into his workplace. The group at the central monitor all turned to look at him with expressions of confusion and concern.

"Naomi!" whimpered a bearded, middle-aged man at the center of the group. Like the others, he wore the white jacket of their official uniform, but there was a T-shirt clearly visible underneath it, and his shorts and sneakers weren't exactly professional either.

Senko Tsunehisa, the chief operations officer of the AllTale Center, was a 57-year-old man who'd somehow managed to avoid growing up. It was part of what let him achieve so many genuinely astonishing scientific feats, to hit on ideas a true adult never could. And at the moment, he was pouting like a cartoon character.

Naomi deeply trusted and respected the man. He was the only mentor Naomi had ever had. He was also a *serious* annoyance when it came to anything outside of work.

"You're here, Naomi!" said the woman seated beside Senko, speaking in Indonesian rather than Japanese. "We've got serious localized damage in the records. We tried using the automatic data repair module, but it can't keep up."

This was Xu Yiyi, Senko's assistant and the project's chief researcher. Quickly tapping her fingers against the table monitor, she called up a summary of the ongoing incident. This woman did the work of three ordinary researchers; she single-handedly made up for Senko's capriciousness and lack of common sense.

"Don't know what caused it, either!" said Senko with a casual shrug. "Any ideas, Naomi?"

For whatever reason, these two had started using Naomi's given name rather than the more professional *Katagaki-san*, and now almost all the other staff members followed their example. It didn't really bother him, but it did feel a bit like he was still back in school.

The two of them looked at him expectantly, but he shook his head rather than replying. The most convenient answer was that he just didn't know what was wrong.

"Let's focus on the problem at hand for now," he said, approaching the monitor table and tapping at the screen, which showed red lines radiating away from a large circle labeled *AllTale* at the center of the display. "Looking at the map, the damaged data seems to be causing cascading damage to other sections of the records. At this rate, the butterfly effect is going to push us past the point of no return. And if we let that happen..."

"The whole simulation collapses," said Senko, scratching his head. Xu didn't say anything, but she was staring intently at the map with a deep frown on her face. It was clear from the display alone that their intricate, infinite-capacity masterpiece was on the brink of a complete system failure.

Senko folded his arms and closed his to eyes think. After a few moments of hesitation, he turned back to face Xu and Naomi. "We need to initiate recovery mode."

The pronouncement elicited a chorus of groans from the other staff members. Everyone in the room was familiar with the procedure, but they'd never had to use it since the AllTale system started running.

Recovery mode involved a temporary shutdown of AllTale's hardware systems, followed by a backup and repair of all the records it preserved. It was a last resort emergency maintenance method, only to be used in a Stage 4 crisis scenario. Even with the staff working at full speed, it would take thousands of hours to complete.

No one objected, despite the grumbles. With a situation this dire unfolding, Senko's decision made sense.

"This way, we'll at least keep the hardware safe, right?" said Senko with a glance around the room, his tone consoling.

The formal order hadn't been issued yet, but Xu was already rising from her chair. "First things first, everyone. We need to retrieve and preserve the records in block format. Then we get the repair started."

"Yeesh, this is going to be a pain," Senko added helpfully with a shrug of his shoulders. He looked at Naomi with an apologetic expression. "Can you get on this right away, Naomi?"

"Of course." As he replied, Naomi reached into his pocket and took out an ID card, clipping it to his shirt. The terminals automatically scanned these cards to authorize access, so he needed to have his on when he was working.

The plastic case still had the word *NAOMI!* scrawled on it in Magic Marker—the remnants of another one of Senko's stupid pranks. He'd been meaning to wipe it off for ages, but never seemed to get around to it.

The card encased inside the holder, on the other hand, was a very professional-looking ID that listed his full name and official title.

AllTale Center

System Management Director
Katagaki Naomi

3.

One of the AllTale center's perks for senior staff was a personal room on site. Naomi had earned one of his own upon his promotion to director.

The room was about 140 square feet and it contained everything he needed: a work desk, bookshelves packed with technical tomes, and a thick blanket for the days when he was forced to sleep at work. At first, he'd tried to keep this room tidy, but by now it had acquired the clutter of a lived-in space.

Naomi picked out a few books from his disorganized shelves. This would be the first time they'd ever run Recovery Mode on the AllTale system, so they'd probably run into unexpected errors. He should prepare as thoroughly as possible.

Once he'd chosen everything he thought he might need, Naomi glanced down. There was a half-open cardboard box sitting partway under his desk; a grimy vest was visible inside it.

It wasn't a particularly fashionable piece of clothing. Exposed electrical wires were taped clumsily to its entire surface, and since he couldn't wash the thing, every inch of it was dirty...but the inside of it was particularly filthy, especially the back.

It wasn't just sweat that had soaked into the fabric. It was blood, and skin, and bits of charred human flesh. The stains had dried out long ago, but they were still disturbingly vivid. Most people would have flinched and looked away with a grimace.

But Naomi just smiled with a far-off look in his eyes.

Reaching down to close the lid, he sealed the box shut with tape and pushed it out of sight entirely. With his books under one arm and his cane in the other, he left his room and headed for the control center.

The preparations for entering Recovery Mode took several hours of feverish work. But even when they were complete, there was no way to tell how smoothly the function would go. The team decided to closely monitor every stage of the process, expecting that they'd need to manually intervene at multiple points along the way.

"We'll start off in Safe Mode and focus on breaking the connections between the records for a while. If things get too out of whack, we'll smooth them out with the Sifter. Once we're done, we'll open up every sector simultaneously."

Senko went on to explain the process step-by-step in detail, then turned back to his desk. "My system sure is a mess, huh?" he murmured with a little laugh.

A message popped up on the Control Center's front monitor to indicate that the preparations were complete, and a dialogue box appeared on Naomi's screen asking him to confirm the initiation of Recovery Mode. As the man responsible for the system's upkeep and maintenance, it was his job to press the start button.

He turned back in his chair, looking to Senko for final

confirmation. With a slightly sad look on his face, the bearded man nodded.

"No way around it, I guess."

Naomi nodded back and reached out toward his monitor. But just as his finger was about to touch the screen, he hesitated.

Memories flashed through his mind in quick succession. He furrowed his brow; these weren't productive thoughts right now. Some things were best forgotten.

The time he'd spent inside AllTale was best forgotten.

For the past three months, he'd carried out an *operation* there. He'd materialized in the simulated world and contacted his younger self. He'd warned the boy of Ichigyou Ruri's accident and told him how to prevent it. He'd trained him extensively, moved him around the board like a pawn, and helped him save the girl he loved.

And then he'd stolen her away.

He'd had no choice—it was the only way to repair her brain, since he needed the quantum record of her consciousness to complement the undamaged areas. The only way to obtain that map was to pluck the data that composed her out of the system entirely. Retrieving data from a quantum computer wasn't as simple as copying a computer file. It required close observation of the AllTale system.

But the more closely quantum data was observed, the more the original was altered. It was impossible to produce a perfect copy; the process would inevitably distort and destroy the original data. So, Ichigyou Ruri disappeared from that world when he retrieved her data. It was an inevitable side effect of the process.

With his mission completed, Naomi left the quantum simulation and returned to reality. The world he'd abandoned still existed inside AllTale, of course. What was happening in there right now? How had it been affected by his actions?

He had no idea. The nature of the system made it impossible to observe clearly from the outside. But even if he couldn't see it now, that world was *real*. The Kyoto he'd spent three months in still existed. So did the people living there.

The Recovery process would erase it completely.

They would retrieve the quantum data from the system and return the AllTale hardware to its initial state. After repairing the records externally, they would be returned to the system. The simulated world inside the machine would be annihilated, piece by piece, and then rebuilt anew.

When he pressed this button, that world would end. With the simulation shut down, his mission would truly be over.

The kid would disappear along with it.

He'd known all this from the start, of course. His actions would leave a lasting impact on the AllTale system, and he'd assumed they might have to do a full Recovery. This was all going more or less as he'd expected.

He *knew* that. His feelings now weren't logical, they were just useless sentiment.

"Naomi?" Senko called dubiously.

Naomi shook his head and pressed the start button.

A long list of steps popped up on the main monitor, and a colored progress bar began to inch forward along the first row. They would need to keep a close eye on things for another ten-odd hours before the automated process could completely take over.

Forcing himself to focus on the task at hand, Naomi looked back down at his monitor. But just then, a hand fell on his shoulder.

"Why don't you go get some rest, Naomi?" said Senko, as casual as ever. Naomi blinked in surprise; the real work was just starting. "I mean, you didn't get any sleep yesterday either, did you?"

"No, but that wasn't work related..."

"I was really happy to hear about your girlfriend, y'know."

A smile spread across Naomi's face despite himself, and he nodded slightly. Senko knew all about Naomi's girlfriend, who'd been in a coma for a decade. From the day Naomi first joined his research lab in college, the two of them had been closer and friendlier than a typical professor and student. The team had slept over at the lab more often than not.

When Naomi graduated, Senko had brought him right into the AllTale Center under his command. The man was more than a mentor or boss to Naomi—he was closer to a father figure.

"Must have been one eeeemotional reunion!" Senko added, sticking out his lower lip and pretending to cry. "Wouldn't be fair to lock you up at work right now. I don't want you telling everyone what a nightmare of a boss I am!"

"I think I'm needed here, though..."

"Not to worry. I can handle ten times your workload, anyway."

Naomi had to laugh at that. It was true, in a sense; he was still a very long way from reaching Senko's level of expertise and knowledge. But the man rarely focused on any given task for very long. Given his short attention span and tendency to goof off, he usually wasn't any more productive than Naomi was.

In other words, the extra work was mostly going to fall into Xu's lap. The way she was scowling at Senko suggested that she knew it, too. That only made him want to laugh harder.

After a moment, Xu let out a small sigh and pointed toward the exit.

Naomi bowed his head gratefully to both of them and took his ID badge off his chest. With a brief apology to the rest of the staff, he hurried out of the Control Center and headed for the elevator.

It was past 8 PM and, outside the center, night had already fallen.

Clutching his cane more tightly than usual, Naomi hurried down the street toward the hospital.

Was she awake right now, or sleeping? Either was fine with him, of course. If she was asleep, it would only be for a few short hours; she'd open her eyes again in the morning. That was *nothing* compared to ten long years.

He realized he was practically bouncing and tried to tamp down on his excitement. As his mind grew calmer, a nagging hint of guilt slipped into his thoughts.

Mentally, he apologized once more. To Senko, to Xu, and to all the coworkers he'd lied to.

And to the boy.

All of this was his fault, but he could never tell them that. He'd keep it locked up in his mind forever and take his secret to the grave.

Calmly, deliberately, Naomi headed for the hospital.

A cold moon hung in the Kyoto sky.

A COLD MOON HUNG IN THE KYOTO SKY.

An unpleasant, sticky wind blew through the city. Thick clouds rolled into view, hiding the moon; before long, they'd covered the entire sky, forming a solid lid over the Uji River.

The people who'd come to see the fireworks were chatting in the distance. Some of them sounded excited, others concerned.

"Was that lightning?"

"Was there an accident?"

None seemed to know what had happened, but most of them weren't too worried. Whatever it was, it was over, and no real damage had been done. Now that the show was over, it was time to go back to their normal lives. Their first priority was to make it back to the station and head home before the trains filled up.

The fireworks were over for the year.

"Sensei?"

Standing alone in the middle of a bridge, Katagaki Naomi called out once again. There was no reply.

He stared up blankly at the sky. His mind couldn't form any coherent thoughts. His brain had been going a mile a minute, but now it felt like it'd shut down completely.

He *wanted* to think, of course. Slowly, with the clumsy ineptitude of a toddler, he pieced words together inside his mind. Nothing was making any sense, but he forced his thoughts forward one step at a time.

Naomi scanned the length of the bridge. Ichigyou Ruri was nowhere to be seen. She'd been standing here moments ago, but now she was gone.

Why? Well, the claws of that crow had surrounded her, transformed into a cage, and disappeared into the sky. It had reminded him a little of the way the fox-masks had teleported them here. Maybe she'd been sent off somewhere else now.

In that case...

"I've got to find them," Naomi muttered softly to himself.

He shuffled one foot forward. He'd meant to take a step, but instead, the sole of his shoe scraped weakly against the stone surface of the bridge.

He was close to one of the bridge's decorative poles, a post of painted wood and metal pointing straight up at the sky. That was convenient. Approaching it, Naomi pressed his right hand to its surface.

He wasn't wearing his glove.

"Huh?"

Right. The glove had sprouted wings and flown away on him. He didn't have the God Hand anymore. It had slipped his mind somehow.

He'd have to find some other way to pursue them, then.

For now, he needed to get moving. He started to walk. There was no point hanging around on this bridge all day.

Where was he supposed to go, though? The station, maybe?

As he thought through his next step, Naomi stepped mindlessly onto the broad steps at the end of the bridge and tripped, tumbling down to the very bottom.

Naomi grimaced in pain as he hit the ground. He'd smacked his arms and legs against the hard stone stairs, and he could tell some of his scrapes were bleeding. He lay still for a moment, spread out like a dead frog. He could hear muttering voices around him—apparently he'd had an audience for his pratfall. How embarrassing.

Naomi tried to pick himself up, but his joints ached and didn't act how he'd expected. Humiliated, desperate, he pressed his hand to the stony ground.

But he didn't have his glove on.

And in this moment, he finally understood.

No train, no bus, no boat could take him where he needed to go. Nothing could take him to where she was.

"Give me *something*," he said, pressing his right hand to the ground.

Nothing emerged.

"Give me *anything*!" he shouted, punching his hand against the unyielding stone. "A plane! A car! A bike! How about an elevator? A flight of stairs? Anything's fine! I don't care!"

He punched the ground again and again. Over and over. But it was still stone. It refused to transform.

"Come on, *please*! Turn into water, I don't care! Just do something!"

A drop of water fell beside Naomi's hand.

Another followed, and then another, plopping softly against the stones. A summer rain fell from the thick clouds above; in no time at all, it grew from a drizzle into a storm.

It was a natural phenomenon, of course. Naomi's hand hadn't produced a single drop of it. An ordinary human hand wasn't capable of something like that.

After a long moment, Naomi forced his aching body to its feet and trudged off through the driving rain.

Deep puddles had formed on the sidewalks, but Naomi rushed straight through them. Muddy water splashed up with every step he took, but what did it matter? His pants and shoes were already soaked through. There wasn't much point going around.

He breathed rapidly, in gasps. It felt like his heart might give out at any moment. But he didn't stop walking. If he slowed down, if he let himself catch his breath, he might start *thinking* again.

He might remember she'd been taken away.

He might remember that Sensei did it.

His chest burned, an unendurable pain that ate him alive

from the inside out. He ran toward Shimogamo, desperately hoping that relief was waiting for him.

Maybe she's back at home right now.

He had no reason to believe it, of course. Why would she disappear into thin air, only to reappear back where she belonged? Still, he headed for her house, clinging to a fantasy.

Through the heavy rain, he finally saw her house come into view some way down the road. He came to a sudden halt, his breath caught in his throat.

The rain was *avoiding* her house.

Naomi opened his mouth, but no sound came out. He looked up into the sky, disbelieving.

The Ichigyou residence was surrounded by a semi-transparent dome made of countless hexagonal panels locked tightly together, colored like a stained-glass window. Particles of light slid around their edges. Sometimes, one of the panels would flash bright red before returning to its semi-transparent state. The rain bounced right off it.

"What *is* this?"

With faltering, hesitant steps, he approached the surface of the dome. As he drew close, one of the hexagonal panels flashed and displayed a message in Japanese.

Major data corruption has been detected in this sector.

This area will remain inaccessible until repairs are complete.

AllTale System

Naomi furrowed his brow. It was the kind of bland error message you'd see when a computer broke down. He could understand what it meant, at least—this area was broken in some way.

But this was Ichigyou Ruri's *home*. How could it be broken?

Naomi's heart thumped painfully in his chest. Suddenly, it all felt horribly real. Sensei had told him everything months ago. He knew what this world was, and he'd thought he understood.

But he hadn't. Not really. Not until this moment.

He could hear the man's voice echoing in his ears.

"You are a record of Katagaki Naomi as he existed in the past."

"So then...I'm..."

"The God Hand works by directly accessing the data AllTale uses to generate this simulation."

Naomi's head spun. The ground beneath him didn't seem *real* anymore. He pressed a hand to his mouth, trying to hold back a wave of nausea.

I'm not real.

I'm just a piece of data in a computer. So is Ruri.

So is this entire world.

Naomi heard a splash behind him, and he spotted something on the other side of the road. It was an oddly shaped humanoid figure wearing a bright yellow belt. And of course, there was a *kitsune* mask covering its face.

But...*why*? It didn't make sense.

Naomi reached up to touch his face. He wasn't wearing those glasses anymore, of course, but these masked things were supposed to be invisible without them. They didn't belong in this world, after all; they were a part of the system that controlled it.

Something clicked in his mind, and he turned back to the dome. Shouldn't that apply to this thing, too? It was clearly part of the AllTale system, so it shouldn't be visible to the naked eye.

Splash.

Spinning back, Naomi saw the fox-mask draw closer. As it strode through the puddles, water splashed up around its feet.

Naomi didn't understand what was going on here, but he could tell it wasn't good. Something had gone very wrong.

Its legs were touching the water. The fox-mask had physically manifested inside this world.

At that moment, he noticed two more approaching him. All three moved toward him at a slow, steady pace, the emotionless eyes of their masks fixed directly on him.

"Go away!" he cried fearfully, thrusting out his arms to ward them off. The hands in front of him were naked...empty. He had no tools or weapons, nothing to use to fight them. And somehow, there were twenty of them approaching now.

"Ah..." His voice trembled, and then broke.

"Aaaaah!"

Screaming, Naomi turned and fled. Driven by sheer terror, he ran without even a glance over his shoulder. He could hear countless footsteps following close behind.

There was a puddle of muddy water inches from Naomi's face. It was nauseating, but he couldn't lift his head away from the ground. He was lying on his stomach underneath a truck.

He'd fled to the north end of Kyoto, not far from the

mountains that encircled the area. The houses were fewer and further between as he ran; there weren't many places to hide out here. Finally cornered by the fox-masks, he had been forced to flee into a field dotted with plastic greenhouses, where he'd slipped under this truck to hide. Now he was trapped down here.

Turning his head as far as he could, he tried to scan the area. The ground was covered in puddles; raindrops rippled their surfaces. A boot slammed down into one, splashing dirty water directly into Naomi's face. He forced himself not to cry out.

The mud around the truck was torn up by countless footprints. There weren't just twenty or thirty of those masked things anymore; more than a hundred pairs of legs walked endlessly around the area, searching in all directions.

Every single one of them was looking for Naomi. He didn't know why, but they'd chased him single-mindedly all the way from Ruri's house.

They moved slowly, so at first he'd thought he could lose them if he ran. But the fox-masks kept popping up out of thin air everywhere he went. It didn't matter how far he fled; they appeared in the middle of the street, inside the houses, and between the trees.

Now they were wandering around only a few feet from Naomi's face. They didn't seem to know where he was, for some reason. None of them bent down to look under the truck.

But there were just too many of them. It had to be a matter of time until they started physically ramming themselves against any nearby objects. Squeezing himself flat against the ground, Naomi quieted his breathing and tried to think. How could he escape?

The question had been running circles around his mind for a while now, but he wasn't coming up with much of anything. No matter how hard he tried to focus, he found his thoughts moving in unproductive directions, seeking escape from this grim reality.

Why did this have to happen?

He'd worked so *hard* these last three months. He'd done what felt right to him. He'd even faced a challenge that felt downright impossible. He'd done it for himself, and for her...and for his mentor.

In classic *Little Match Girl* style, his mind pulled up the happiest memories it could find. He remembered the day he met Ichigyou Ruri, and the time they'd spent together in the library committee. He remembered sitting next to her at the front desk and reading quietly together. He remembered pulling the cart full of books along the road, sweating through his shirt.

He remembered how he'd opened up to her about the books he liked, and how she'd understood. He remembered the day they started going out.

He remembered how *certain* he'd been about all the happy days ahead of them.

Naomi's imagination pulled him away from reality, made him forget about the masked things hunting for him. He fled into his mind, into his happiest fantasies.

He remembered a few things that *didn't* involve Ruri, too. His first encounter with Sensei at Fushimi Inari, and the agreement they'd reached on the rooftop. His training sessions with the magic glove, and their long discussions, planning out his romantic strategy. The help he'd finally given Naomi that night when he replicated the books.

Sensei had taught him so many things and helped him grow like a brother. He'd been a real mentor, a true friend.

Naomi's face crumpled and bitter tears ran down his face. His hands clawed at the mud as he tried to squeeze them into fists.

It was a lie. It was all one big lie.

All of it was fake—his kindness, his sternness, his concern. There was no hate in Naomi's heart, only pain and sadness that he'd been deceived, and that Sensei was gone. He was heartbroken.

He'd lost everything he cared about.

A croaking sob forced itself out of his throat, and his tears disappeared into the muddy water.

He could see the legs of the wandering fox-masks reflected in that same puddle. For some reason, they'd stopped moving. Naomi tilted his head to look up from the ground. The countless legs were *all* frozen in place. He watched them uncertainly.

Without the constant drumming of the masked things' footsteps, an eerie silence had fallen on the area. In that silence, Naomi could just make out a faint sound from very far away.

Is that a siren?

It sounded a lot like the alarm the local government played over the city's loudspeakers during emergency evacuations drills or to announce a missing person. Naomi thought he could hear a voice as well, but the words were muffled and hard to hear from underneath this truck.

Listening closely, he managed to pick out a phrase or two. He thought he heard the words "Recovery Mode."

A bright light flashed, and Naomi covered his face reflexively.

Squinting, he peered out from underneath the truck. One thing's *kitsune* mask was shining. In its very center, something round, bright, and yellow had appeared—it almost looked like the warning lights set up near road construction.

It was an *eye*—a single, shining eye grown in the center of the mask. Or perhaps a third, if you counted the two slender ones on the mask itself.

One by one, the same eyes appeared on every mask Naomi could see, like a chain reaction. Simultaneously, their hands all began to glow.

Naomi had to smile at that. It was a weak, miserable smile, but what else was he supposed to do?

It was the God Hand. The familiar glove had appeared on every one of the fox-masks' hands.

One of the things knelt down and pressed its hands to the ground. A large section of soil reshaped itself into a neat cube and promptly disappeared, leaving nothing behind.

Naomi understood what had happened. He knew how the God Hand worked inside and out, after all. That thing had just rewritten the world, converting a piece of the ground into pure information. The dirt hadn't been replaced with air or turned transparent; it had been *erased*.

That thing had turned *something* into *nothing*.

Suddenly, the entire army of masked things erupted into frantic motion. Instead of their slow shuffle, they ran rapidly around the area, slamming themselves at every object in their paths. Some leapt at the ground itself. Others attacked the greenhouses. Some threw their hands at the walls of nearby houses. And with their gloves, they changed all of it to nothing.

They were erasing Kyoto. They were deleting this entire world.

Everything suddenly got much brighter, and Naomi realized that the truck he'd been hiding under had been erased. A three-eyed fox-mask was staring right down at him.

Naomi thrashed frantically into action. Wriggling like a bug on its back, he rolled over and crawled away on all fours through the mud. He slipped on the slick soil but somehow managed to scramble to his feet; an instant later, he was running blindly away, as fast as his legs would carry him. But the fox-masks were running too, moving just as wildly.

There were hundreds of them now, or even thousands. They weren't pursuing Naomi specifically anymore, though; now, they were after *everything* that made up this entire world, Naomi included. Sprinting in every direction, they destroyed everything they touched like a rampaging army of bulldozers. Bit by bit, the world was leveled, reduced to nothing.

The all-engulfing wave of masked things was close behind him. Naomi was out of options—all he could do now was run.

Naomi trudged up a gentle slope, walking along a road that

led through the mountains surrounding Kyoto. There were fewer houses here, and much more greenery. No one else was on the street, and he hadn't seen a single car on the road so far.

All alone, Naomi dragged his aching, soaked legs forward. His drenched clothes were heavy with water; they dragged him down like chains.

He wasn't moving quickly now, too exhausted to force himself to run. Still, the fox-masks hadn't caught up to him yet.

Most of their army had headed toward the dense city center, rather than spreading out to the fringes. Their goal was to erase everything, so maybe they were drawn to areas crowded with objects and people. If that was true, they'd probably wouldn't get to the mountains for a bit. If Naomi dragged himself out into the woods, he might be able to hide for a little while.

And after that...

His line of thought ran aground. There was no way to complete that sentence. He knew what was coming in the end...eventually, there'd be nowhere left to run.

Naomi's legs slowed to a halt. He looked up at the dark, cloudy night sky through half-closed eyes.

In the distance, another siren blared out.

Naomi's eyes snapped open, and he forced himself to listen closely. This was the second siren of the evening. Once again, it came from somewhere far away; once again, he heard some sort of announcement playing. But he'd put more distance between himself and the city now, so he couldn't make out a single word.

All he could do was wait anxiously, listen to the blaring sound, and see what happened next.

A pebble rolled across the ground toward Naomi.

He looked down at it curiously; it seemed to be moving all on its own. Before long, other little rocks began to follow its example.

After a moment, he figured out what was happening. The slope he was walking up was *growing steeper*.

A rock the size of a baseball came tumbling down as the road rose up in front of him. A moment ago, it had been no steeper than a wheelchair ramp; now it was more like the ramp up a pedestrian bridge. Before Naomi could even try to flee, it turned into an asphalt slide.

"Ah! Aaah!"

Naomi fell to his hands and knees, clutching at the ground, fighting against the growing force of gravity. But it proved pointless; the road just kept rising up and up.

The force of gravity overwhelmed that of friction, and his body began to slide downward along the slick, wet road. He couldn't stop his fall, just slid faster and faster as the road grew steeper.

Throwing the weight of his body to one side, Naomi managed to change course slightly. Sliding diagonally toward the side of the road, he tried to grab hold of the guardrail, but his rain-slick hands slipped off. Still, he kept reaching out for it, trying to at least slow himself down a little. The road was as steep as a ski slope now; his arms and legs flapped desperately against it.

Naomi found himself approaching a curve in the road. The guardrail he'd been sliding alongside was now a metal bar directly in his path, and his shoulder slammed into it, sending a shock through his entire body. Ignoring the pain as best he could, he caught hold of a support post, finally pausing his descent. There was a streetlight standing right next to the post; Naomi reached out to grab it, then wriggled his way onto its thicker pole, finally regaining his balance.

This new perch made the situation terribly clear.

Naomi was balanced on the side of a light pole, his arms and legs wrapped around it. The ground was a vertical wall.

Stunned, he looked *over* at the sky.

It wasn't above him anymore. It was straight off to the side—a great wall of dark clouds, stretching out vertically in the distance.

In the middle of that wall was a hole.

The dirty gray clouds had formed a kind of funnel around it, like an antlion's trap. At the center was a small, black spot that Naomi couldn't see inside—from here, it looked pure black.

Objects soared through the air toward it, and it sucked them in. First, Naomi saw it eat a car. Then a vending machine. Then a bus. Then a building. All sort of things flew off the surface of the city and disappeared into that hole.

The light pole he was sitting on, which had been horizontal, began to bend.

Everything finally clicked into place.

The world had been bent at a 90-degree angle. Soon, it would be bent to *180 degrees*. The ground would be up and the sky would be down. Before long, everything in this world would fall into the sky.

They would be shaken down, bit by bit, like flour falling through a sifter. For a moment he wondered what they'd do about objects that were solidly attached to the ground; but then he remembered that the fox-masks had been rampaging through the city for some time now. They'd probably been cutting everything loose, ensuring everything could fall into that hole.

It felt horribly plausible, considering what he'd seen. This was how everything was going to end, with the entire city vanishing into that tiny dot. It was all going to go. The buildings, the trees, even the soil.

And, of course, him.

I'm going to disappear. I get it now. I'm...

"I'm going to die."

Somehow, it felt more real when he spoke the words out loud.

As a kid, Naomi had once broken his favorite toy robot. He'd been trying to turn it back into a car, but it got stuck, and when he tried to force it one of the legs snapped right off. It was immediately clear that it couldn't be repaired, no matter what.

What he'd felt in that moment was the closest comparison he could think of to what he felt now—that feeling of inevitability.

Naomi began to cry. He blubbered like a child at the overwhelming pain of it all. It was just too much to bear. And the more he cried, the more miserable he felt.

But what else was he supposed to do? It was over. It was all over. There wasn't anything to be done.

That toy *was* broken.

And he *was* going to die.

"Ichigyou-san..." He called out to the girl he loved, who he knew he'd never see again. His pointless cries disappeared into the hole, along with everything else.

Then, as he stared at it through his tears, something occurred to him. He'd seen something like this before. But where? When?

Right...when Sensei took her away...

The crow's claws had rained down from above, forming an octagonal cage. And that cage had flown up into the sky.

It had *pierced* the sky, opening a hole that looked just like the one he was staring at now. And if she'd gone into that hole... maybe she was waiting on the other side of it?

There was a low, loud crash as a large truck collided with a small building in midair, breaking both apart. A moment later, they were both sucked into the hole.

Naomi shook his head fiercely, the blood draining from his face.

"I can't!"

The idea was ridiculous. Jumping into that hole would be *suicide*. And there wasn't even any guarantee that it connected to wherever Ruri had gone. He had zero evidence—the thought was just a convenient fantasy.

He wasn't living in a story. Things wouldn't work out so neatly.

Katagaki Naomi avoided taking risks. He never threw himself at a challenge unless he knew the outcome in advance.

Those were the rules he'd lived by since the day he was born. He'd never changed. He *couldn't* change. Even after meeting Sensei, he'd simply put his faith in the *Ultimate Manual*, letting it give him all the answers. He'd never broken his rules, not even once.

Oh. Wait.

The image of a book had flashed into his mind—a stained old novel with a nice illustration on the cover, frayed corners, and a library card in the back.

He'd made that book, hadn't he?

Yeah. I remember now. I pulled it off, didn't I? I had no idea how it might turn out, and Sensei told me to stop, but I did it anyway.

Just that once, I made my own decision.

Naomi looked up from his creaking perch. The world suddenly looked oddly clear to him, like the feeling when your head clears up after a cold.

He rose to his feet atop the slanting light pole like a gymnast on a balance beam.

And then...

He jumped into the sky.

5.

INSIDE THE HOLE, Naomi saw a jellyfish.

He was in outer space. It was made of water, and every possible color all at once.

Something big swallowed him up. He was broken into chunks, and every piece of him caught fire.

Once he was nice and smooth, he was scattered into bits.

Someone was looking him in the eye. Naomi wanted to say hello, but he couldn't.

There wasn't any *Naomi* left to speak.

6.

SOMETIMES, A SHINTO SHRINE has a particular kind of stage, the kind used for Noh theater, *mamemaki* rituals, and other similar events. Naomi had lived in Kyoto his whole life, so he'd seen a lot of shrines for a boy his age. He recognized that he was standing on one of those stages almost immediately.

Naomi glanced around him. There were two white mounds of sand just outside the stage, on opposite ends. They seemed familiar, but he couldn't remember where he'd seen them before. They were definitely from a shrine in the city, though.

He looked around again, hoping for another hint. But apart from the mounds of sand, the space around him looked like heaven, or maybe hell. Possibly outer space.

Slowly, something dawned on him.

"Am I dead?" he murmured sadly to no one in particular.

"No, you're not."

Naomi flinched backward. There was a three-legged crow standing on the floor right in front of him.

Once he got over his initial surprise, Naomi stepped toward it cautiously. It was *that* crow, the one that had turned into a glove. Or maybe it was a glove that turned into a crow. Whatever. Either way, it had betrayed him.

And just to make things even more unsettling, it was *speaking* to him.

"Uh, you can talk?" Naomi asked.

"Yes, I can," the crow replied in a calm, businesslike manner. Its voice sounded like a woman's, but its tone was oddly flat; it reminded Naomi of a prerecorded menu on a corporate support line. "I can also answer your questions. To repeat, you are *not* currently dead."

"Oh. Really?"

"Additionally, you may consider me your ally."

Naomi looked at the bird dubiously. It was a little hard to take the thing at its word, especially since it had backstabbed him not too long ago.

On closer inspection, though, he realized that this crow had a small patch of blond hair on the crown of its head. The crow he knew had been completely black; maybe this was a different bird entirely. Not that he had any way to be sure.

"Katagaki Naomi," the bird said; apparently it wasn't going to give him time to think this over. Staring at him with its glassy, unreadable eyes, it continued, "You're going to take Ichigyou Ruri back with your own hands."

7.

"I'M GOING to *what*?" Naomi responded stupidly.

"Take back Ichigyou Ruri," the bird replied, ignoring his obvious confusion. "The world has been thrown off balance. To correct this, the Homeostatic System will likely attempt to erase her. You need to prevent this. Return her to her rightful place in the world where she belongs."

"That's, uh, easy for you to say..." Naomi couldn't make any sense of this, and this bird didn't seem to want to help him understand. He had no idea what to think.

Ruri had been stolen from him. That was true.

He wanted to see her again. He'd jumped willingly into that hole on the off chance it would take him to her. But he hadn't really thought through what might come next.

He knew what he *wanted*. He wanted to bring her back, to see her again, to wrap his arms around her.

But...

Naomi stared down at his hands. "I'm completely powerless."

"Incorrect," the crow replied calmly. "You have a power all your own. One you developed through steady, focused practice." The bird wasn't sitting in front of Naomi anymore. Startled, he looked around and spotted it flitting through the air some distance away.

Suddenly, it banked in midair and began to dive straight toward Naomi at an incredible speed.

Naomi threw up his arms reflexively to block the attack. The bird slammed into him a split second later; but strangely, there was no pain whatsoever.

Instead, there was a glove on his right hand. Naomi stared at it blankly. It wasn't the same as his old one—this one was pure white.

"What are you?" he murmured in disbelief.

"Just a crow," his glove responded. "A crow that watched you work very hard for the last three months."

Naomi felt something *surge* out of his glove. He couldn't see it or hear it, but it was enough. He understood now.

He could reach her with his own hands.

"Katagaki Naomi-san," the glove continued in its voicemail-menu voice. "Do you want a girlfriend?"

I've heard that one before...

This time, the answer was easy.

"Yes!"

Naomi's hand closed around something of its own volition. He'd grabbed hold of a shining cord—like the Spider's Thread from that Akutagawa story, only much thicker and sturdier. Looking up, he saw that the roof of the stage had disappeared. The cord stretched up endlessly into the heavens.

Naomi gave it a great, powerful tug. In response, the cord yanked him up; his body soared into the sky like a firework.

He rocketed through the sky, past the stars, past outer space itself, and into a perfectly vertical rainbow-colored tunnel. The great string guided him into its mouth. He flew up and up through it.

The journey felt like it took years, or perhaps seconds. Maybe both.

Naomi's body shrunk into a tiny speck. The border between him and the world grew vague and uncertain. Things were passing *through* him in a constant, chaotic torrent: energy, objects, people.

And at the end of that great river, Katagaki Naomi *fused* with himself.

HELLO WORLD
THE NOVEL

CHAPTER SIX

1.

AN AIR CONDITIONER hummed faintly.

Naomi hadn't heard this exact sound before, but it was also painfully familiar. Two contradictory thoughts coexisted in his mind. He had merged, blended with someone else; there was a second Naomi now inside him. It was a peculiar feeling, to say the least.

Gradually, he took stock of his surroundings. He was in a hospital room. There was a large, bulky bed at its center, with an array of machines standing at its side. The window on the wall had its blinds down; great strings of folded paper cranes hung next to it, with a banner that read *From the Nishiki High Library Committee.*

In the bed itself lay Ichigyou Ruri.

She looked the same, just as she had when she disappeared into the sky after the fireworks festival. But this wasn't something that Naomi had ever experienced. This had to be a little while after her *accident*—the accident he'd prevented.

He was seeing Sensei's memories.

"I had shelf-sorting duty today," someone said in Naomi's voice. He'd felt his own mouth moving, like his body had a mind of his own. "I've gotten a lot more practice, I guess. I managed to get it done before four this time. It goes quicker when I'm working by myself." Naomi felt himself smiling slightly, thinking about their strange system when they shelved books together.

Naomi sat in a dark hall.

With no warning, he'd been brought somewhere else entirely—to a different place and time. But he immediately knew where he was and what he was doing there. The knowledge was sitting right there in his brain.

This was the Academic Hall at Kyoto College. He was a student here.

There was a slideshow on the big screen up front, which was why the lights were down. An older man with shaggy hair and a big beard gave a lecture to Naomi and the other students around him. Naomi had seen the man before, not too long ago, when he took that tour of the Chronicle Kyoto Project Center.

A video started on the screen. A white mouse appeared, apparently from some experiment or another. The animal was deep asleep, its mouth half-open; it almost looked dead. There were a bunch of wires or cords sticking out of its head.

After a moment, the small lights attached to the wires began to flicker.

The exhausted mouse instantly awoke, pushing itself up off

the ground with surprising steadiness. Naomi heard murmurs of surprise from the audience.

At that same moment, he *felt* something new. It was a mixture of emotions, too complex to reduce to a single word, but very, *very* powerful. There was astonishment, and joy, and eagerness. His mind raced, jumping between all sorts of possibilities.

But there was also guilt and shame.

Naomi understood all of it. Sensei's feelings were *his* feelings now. He knew the man's thoughts as clearly as his own.

The presentation on the screen switched over to the next slide, displaying the title of the lecture:

A Practical Application of Quantum Recording: Complementing Nervous System Regeneration via Quantum Imaging of the Brain

Prof. Senko Tsunehisa

Naomi sat in a laboratory.

This was Professor Senko's lab at the university, and Sensei had his own desk there. It was covered in piles of thick, intimidating books.

The professor's research was unbelievably advanced. Naomi had to throw himself completely into his studies if he wanted to make sense of it. He slept in his chair here most nights; whenever he was conscious, he studied with ferocious intensity. He was learning all about Quantum Recording technology and the Kyoto Recording Project.

About AllTale, in other words.

He'd decided on the path he wanted to take. He knew how

he would spend his years in college, where he would work after he graduated, and the career he would pursue. He had a clear vision of how he needed to spend the next few years and the hurdles he would need to clear.

All he had to do was follow through.

He was sleeping less and less these days and eating only when strictly necessary. He knew he didn't have much time, so he gave up completely on having a normal life.

The hurdles he had to make it over were very, very tall. He couldn't afford to waste a single minute.

A brand-new wooden name tag slipped onto its hook on the wall. The characters for Katagaki Naomi carved into its surface.

Sensei stood in a room deep underground, far below the public Chronicle Kyoto Project offices. This was the Control Room of the AllTale Center, the heart of their secret project.

Naomi was twenty-two years old, and he'd successfully secured a job at the AllTale Center immediately after graduating college. His personal connection to Professor Senko had been invaluable, of course; but to earn a staff position on an enormous international enterprise like this, he'd had to pass many extremely difficult examinations and earn all sorts of technical qualifications. This place employed some of the world's foremost scientists and technicians. An ordinary college graduate couldn't exactly expect to get an interview.

But Naomi was far from ordinary. He'd structured his entire life around making it here. He'd thrown everything else aside. And even though his name was now hanging on the wall, that wasn't the goal line. He was only halfway through this marathon, at best.

Naomi gazed at the wooden tag for a moment, contemplating the future. He was interrupted by a blow to the back of his head. Turning around, he found that *someone* had flown a drone directly into it. The bearded culprit was standing across the room with a controller in his hand, guffawing loudly.

This was the man he needed to catch up with.

Senko Tsunehisa was the driving force behind the AllTale Center, the nucleus that held it all together. Naomi needed to become his right-hand man. He needed to rise up the ranks to a senior position; but more importantly, he had to become genuinely invaluable to Senko. He had to become the man's partner. It was the only way to secure an unshakable position inside this project.

To make that happen, he needed to get results. He needed to keep at his studies and his research. He needed to accomplish things no one else could manage.

There was no time to slow down yet. No time to rest.

A slightly worn wooden name tag slipped onto its hook on the wall. The characters for his name were carved into its surface, and beneath them was the freshly cut phrase *System Management Director*.

Sensei was already in conversation with Professor Senko and Xu Yiyi as he entered the now-familiar Control Center. The three of them were working on their latest revision to the Center's formal business plan.

He was the professor's right hand. Xu was his left.

Four years had passed since Naomi first stepped into this room. In that time, the three of them had solved all sorts of seemingly impossible problems together. The entire staff now recognized them as the heart of the AllTale project.

Naomi had risen quickly up the ranks. This place ran on purely meritocratic principles; those who demonstrated particular talent earned their promotions very quickly. But everyone on the staff here was talented in their own way, of course. There were probably others with more raw technical skill than Naomi.

And yet, he had leapfrogged them all and earned the director role. There wasn't anything strange about it, really. He'd just done *everything* it took to get the job.

Naomi flashed his ID card at the wall-mounted camera. It beeped at him softly, and the doors that had been closed to him four years ago slid softly open.

Inside, the AllTale system itself was waiting for him.

Back in his personal room, Naomi began to undress.

When he was promoted to director, he'd been granted this private space within the laboratory itself. This was another crucial aspect of his plan. Accessing the system externally would have amplified the risks. He needed to be physically close, where the security was laxer, and he needed a place where he could be alone.

Naomi tossed his shirt aside, leaving him naked from the waist up. In its place, he slipped on a black vest. The contactless nerve transducers mounted on the inside pressed coldly against his back. It had naked electrical wires taped to the outside, and a single cable ran down to the PC under Sensei's desk.

Sensei lowered himself carefully into his chair and focused on the monitor. The heartbeat display in one corner of the screen indicated that he was intensely anxious.

This would to be his first trial run.

Naomi nodded firmly to himself. His theories were solid. He'd thrown his equipment together quickly, but it met the minimum requirements. It should work. He should be able to get in.

He reached out with his pointer finger and tapped the enter key.

"Gaaah!"

Sensei's body jerked up out of the chair. On pure reflex, he tore off the vest, then he fell to the floor and rolled back and forth in agony. The smell of charred flesh filled the room.

He'd burned his back terribly.

The injured area stretched from just below his neck all the way down to his waist. Everywhere the nerve transducers had been touching him, his skin was burnt and discolored. The blood vessels in his back pulsed fiercely; the intense initial pain gradually gave way to steady, vicious throbbing.

Grabbing hold of his chair, Naomi managed to pull himself up off the ground. There was an error message on his computer monitor: *Timeout. Connection broken.*

For a moment, he felt pure despair. But it faded quickly.

He'd never expected success to come easily. The AllTale was

a system of literally infinite complexity. An ordinary person like Katagaki Naomi couldn't expect to truly understand it on a theoretical level.

He wasn't a genius like Senko Tsunehisa. There would be no shortcuts, no quick victories. This would be a process of trial and error. He would run through experiment after experiment, enduring all the consequences, until he finally succeeded.

That wasn't a problem, really. It was how he made it this far.

With a red pen, Naomi drew an X in the first square on his table of experiments—driving his first peg into the side of the mountain he would climb.

"It's pretty tricky," Sensei said quietly. "Senko-san did create the AllTale system, but there are some aspects of it no one really understands, you know? It works, but we're not completely sure how."

There was no reply, only the humming of the room's air conditioner.

"Writing down all those X's kind of reminds me of the old days, though." Naomi kept speaking, anyway. He didn't care if she couldn't hear him—he wanted to talk to her anyway.

"Remember when we were collecting donations for that used book sale? There was that calendar counting down to the day of the event and everything. We hadn't collected many books, and we started getting antsy..." Sensei's chest throbbed slightly as he spoke those words. The memories were still a little bitter, even if time had softened them. "I guess they all burned up in the end, though."

Disparate memories mingled in Naomi's mind.

He saw Sensei's memories of those events: the fire, the charred books, and the canceled book sale. He didn't have a magic glove, so there wasn't anything he could do about it. He'd just pushed through the pain as best he could.

"Talking to you makes me remember all sorts of things, you know. Remember that time in April—"

Opening a brand-new notebook, Sensei wrote down a date years in the past.

Naomi sat in his personal room in the lab, working on a journal of sorts. It wasn't easy going. He paused between every sentence, furrowing his brow and thinking hard.

What happened on that day again? What exactly was I doing?

When a memory popped into his mind, he jotted it down on a notecard. Once he had enough of those, he transferred them into his notebook, then started working on the next day.

He was creating the *Ultimate Manual.*

It was a retrospective diary of sorts, starting the day he met Ichigyou Ruri and ending with her accident. He recorded every bit of information he could recall about everything that happened over those weeks and months.

Sensei was going to revisit the past—or, rather, a record of it as it existed inside AllTale. Once he made it inside, this notebook would prove extremely useful. His knowledge from the future would be essential to saving her life.

He scribbled down everything he could recall on the notecards, even details that seemed meaningless: what he'd eaten, whether he'd taken a bath or not. Sometimes these little facts would lead him to a more important memory. Better to be thorough now than regret his sloppiness when it was too late.

Slowly, bit by bit, he pieced together the story of their time together like a puzzle.

Remembering her put a smile on his face. Making that notebook was a lot of fun.

Naomi hit the enter key. This would be the 140th experiment.

It was another failure.

Sensei tumbled from his chair. He was used to the pain by now; by the time he hit the floor, he was already thinking about what he'd tweak for next time.

Reaching up to grab his chair, he tried to stand...

He couldn't.

Naomi pulled himself into a sitting position with his arms and stared down at his legs. He tried to spread them apart and his right leg kicked out to one side.

His left leg didn't move an inch.

The air conditioner was spitting out warm air today.

"They call it monoplegia, I guess. My left leg's permanently paralyzed." The sheaf of medical documents clipped to the hospital bed swayed slightly in the current. Outside the window, snow was falling.

"I'm glad it was just a leg, though," Naomi continued quietly. "If I lost an arm, it would have slowed everything down a lot more."

There was no reply.

"Also, it affected my nerves. That means I'm getting closer. I'll have to be careful to avoid any more accidents like this...but once I dig through the data from that experiment, I should be almost ready."

Naomi's gaze dropped to the floor.

After a moment, he spoke again—not to Ruri, or to anyone else. Not even to himself.

"God, I hope so." He paused for a moment, his voice even softer. "I miss her *so* much."

Sensei hit the enter key.

Another failure.

Naomi hit the enter key.

Another failure.

Sensei hit the enter key.

Another failure.

The 336th experiment.

Naomi hit the enter key.

The world went white before his eyes. There was a flash of light; an instant later, he was flying through a rainbow tunnel at a ferocious, terrifying speed.

When he emerged on the other side, the first thing he saw was a long chain of *torii* gates.

He couldn't stop. He was thrown out of the tunnel at the

same velocity he'd traveled through it. The world spun violently as he flew through the red gates.

As he finally started to slow...

Naomi saw *himself* standing on the stone path.

2.

SENSEI OPENED HIS EYES.

He was sitting in the waiting area of a hospital hallway. A glance at the clock told him he'd nodded off for five minutes or so.

In that brief time, he'd had a dream. He'd seen flashes of memory, from the distant past to the present, and he'd dreamed about Naomi.

He'd tried to shake the boy off, but he couldn't get rid of him that easily. He'd probably remember Naomi until the day he died. Naomi would keep glaring at him resentfully forever. He couldn't exactly want him to stop, either. The boy had every right.

He deserved this. And worse.

"Katagaki-san," called the nurse, her face bright with happiness. "She's awake now."

3.

ICHIGYOU RURI GAZED down at her hands. Her wrists were so terribly thin.

It felt like looking at a stranger's body.

She was sitting up in her hospital bed for the first time in years, but the expression on her face wasn't exactly cheerful. From the moment she woke up two days earlier, she had been thinking constantly, trying to understand what had happened to her.

Ruri glanced across the room. At the side of her bed, a young man with a cane artfully arranged a bouquet of flowers with his one free hand. Most of what she'd heard so far had come from him, and from her doctor at this hospital.

They told her that she'd been struck by lightning at a fireworks show ten years ago, and that she'd been in a coma ever since. They told her it was now 2037, and she was twenty-six years old.

The young man said he was Katagaki Naomi, and that he was twenty-six as well.

It was all very hard to believe. It was the kind of story you might find in a novel, but certainly not in real life. How had she suddenly recovered after spending ten years in a coma? The doctors just called it a miracle, which didn't answer any of her questions.

Mentally, Ruri was still a sixteen-year-old girl. She didn't remember anything from the long period of time when she'd been sleeping. But she could remember events from a decade in the past as if they'd happened yesterday. She'd been a member of the library committee. They'd just held a used book sale.

And she'd just started dating Naomi.

Their relationship had only just started, and it wasn't

particularly different from their friendship. They hadn't even gone out anywhere together yet.

Well, supposedly they'd gone to a fireworks festival together, but Ruri couldn't remember anything about it. The doctor had said it was perfectly normal for her memories from right before the accident to be vague. She considered this, and found that there *were* a few small, fragmentary images lurking in a quiet corner of her mind.

She remembered a bridge, swirling clouds, and winds as intense as a hurricane. And she remembered Naomi performing some sort of magic spell.

Ruri had to assume that she'd dreamed that part; it was just too unrealistic and bizarre. But when the doctor insisted she'd gone to the Uji River, she couldn't help tying that to these strange memories.

She was confused, of course, but it hadn't taken long for her to accept her new reality. This hospital room had all the proof she needed. When she looked in the mirror, she saw herself ten years older. When she looked at her arms, she saw how thin they had grown. There was no point arguing with the facts or insisting this wasn't *really* her body. It was the one she had now. If she wanted to object, she'd have to use its mouth to do so.

This wasn't an illusion or a dream. This was who she was now.

There was a small *thunk* from the far side of the room. The young man had finally set down his vase of flowers on the windowsill. Smiling gently at her, he walked over and sat down at her bedside, leaning his cane against the railing.

He'd told her that he'd been in an accident of his own at some point in the last decade. His left leg had been paralyzed in a car crash. The practiced way he moved around with his cane suggested that he'd been coping with the consequences for a while.

That wasn't the only thing that had changed about him, of course; he looked very different now. He was a good foot taller than before, and his once-childish face had matured. There were dark circles under his eyes that looked like they'd been there for quite some time.

Still, Ruri had recognized him instantly.

There was no doubt in her mind—she could still see traces of the boy she'd known. He still had that little scar on his forehead, too—the one she'd noticed when he fell asleep before the used book sale.

It was Katagaki Naomi, now a decade older than she'd known him. And she was ten years older than she'd known herself. It still felt something like a dream, but she had to admit it was true. This was her reality, and she couldn't choose another.

"Do you—"

Ruri looked up at the sound of Naomi's voice, meeting his gaze. He had a strange little half-smile on his face; he still had a bit of that adolescent awkwardness about him, apparently.

"Do you remember the fireworks we saw that night?"

Ruri shook her head. She remembered very little from that outing.

"That's all right," he replied gently. It made Ruri feel a little guilty. She wished she could answer otherwise.

A small dark spot appeared on her bedsheet. Another followed a moment later.

Naomi was crying.

It startled her, probably because this was the first time she'd seen a grown man cry. Even knowing he was Naomi, it was still a shock.

"I missed you so much," he said, his voice cracking with emotion. "I waited for you, you know. All this time."

The tears kept falling, one after another.

It was the push she'd needed to strengthen her resolve. She was going to make the best of this. She would make a life for herself in this unfamiliar world, and she was going to repay him, as best she could, for his kindness and his loyalty.

She still felt anxious and uncertain. There would no doubt be all sorts of problems to overcome. But she would face them as best she could, with his help.

His tears were real, so she decided to trust him.

Ruri felt something touch her hand; he'd reached out to take it with his own. She accepted it and squeezed his hand back.

Maybe they'd held hands on their way to the fireworks festival. But if so, she didn't remember it. As far as she was concerned, this was a first for them.

His crumpled, tearful face drew slowly closer. Ruri was a little frightened, but she pushed that feeling down and squeezed his hand harder.

It's all right, she told herself. *It's him. It's Katagaki-san.*

"That book..." she said. It startled her as much as him—it

felt like her mouth had moved on its own as soon as the words popped into her mind. It was something she remembered clearly from before the accident. Something she'd seen on the day of that used book sale.

That mysterious novel he'd found. The one with her name in the back.

Their book.

"What book...?" he murmured.

Ruri's hand jerked up out of his on pure reflex. She placed both her hands on his chest and pushed him away with what little strength she could muster, sending him back into his chair.

Everything went pure white.

"You're lying." Ruri didn't understand why she was saying this. And yet, it felt *true*.

"You're not Katagaki-san."

4.

NAOMI'S MIND shut down. The meaning what she'd just said wouldn't register.

"You're lying."

Lying? About what?

He *was* Katagaki Naomi. He'd been Katagaki Naomi from the day he was born. Who else could he possibly be?

He bit his lip, his body trembling. He knew what she really meant.

He *was* himself. Katagaki Naomi was his name. But for her, there was another Katagaki Naomi.

Naomi's heart thudded painfully in his chest. His mind raced wildly. He needed to calm down first, then calmly analyze the situation and find a way to resolve it.

She'd called him a liar. There had to be a reason. But judging from the expression on her face, she wasn't entirely confident in what she'd just said. She was still uncertain, so she hadn't made her mind up for good.

He just had to tip the scales back toward him.

He had plenty of material to help him do this. His words would be reinforced by the tangible, physical reality of the world they lived in. There was only one Katagaki Naomi here, and the boy she remembered was nothing but a quantum record inside a computer system.

He could bluff his way through this. He had no choice but to try. Long ago, he'd resolved to make a future for the two of them, no matter what it took.

Suddenly, the door leading to the hallway slid loudly open. Naomi and Ruri both turned toward it.

There was a figure in a *kitsune* mask standing just outside the room.

CHAPTER SEVEN

1.

"WHAT?" Naomi choked out.

The thing was staring in at them from the hospital's hallway. It was instantly recognizable, with its oddly shaped humanoid body, road construction outfit, yellow safety vest, black boots...and the *kitsune* mask.

It was an avatar of the Homeostatic System, an entity from the AllTale's quantum-record world.

These things only existed inside the simulation. It wasn't *possible* for it to be present in the real world.

In the bed beside him, Ruri screamed.

He could hear more footsteps in the hallway, and a second fox-mask appeared behind the first, followed quickly by two more. In only a few moments, there was a swarm of them.

A strange shadow fell across the room. Naomi's head jerked around to the window.

One of the masked things was clinging to the glass from the outside like a lizard. A moment later, there were four of them, then eight, then sixteen. Within seconds, they had covered every inch of the enormous window.

This can't be happening, Naomi thought. *They can't be here. It makes no sense! It's insane!*

But even as he tried to deny what he was seeing, the scientist inside him was steadily, inexorably piecing the facts together.

"This world is a complete, perfect copy of reality, preserved inside the AllTale system."

"Since this world is your reality, you can't tell it's simulated."

His own words guided him to the truth.

"Oh my God...is this...?"

He couldn't believe it...but it didn't matter what he believed.

The lead fox-mask began to sway slightly back and forth. Then, all at once, they poured into the hospital room. The first made a beeline for Ruri's bed, ignoring Naomi completely.

"Stop it!"

Naomi lashed out, sending it sprawling off to one side. But the second thing in line followed close behind, aiming for Ruri as well.

Grabbing his cane, Naomi punched the second attacker before it could reach her. But as he turned toward the third, a great gloved hand smacked into the side of his face and sent him tumbling to the ground.

One of the bulky fox-masks landed on top of him, pressing him against the cold tile floor with enormous force. The damn thing was *heavy*. He thrashed, trying to knock it off him. But it was larger and heavier than him, and one of his legs was disabled—it only took one of those creatures to keep him pinned.

Having dealt with their only obstacle, the fox-masks returned to their task. The first in line leapt up onto Ruri's bed, straddling her slender body.

Naomi struggled frantically, but it was no use.

More of the fox-masks gathered around the bed, seizing her limbs and holding them down. As she lay there, totally immobilized, the one above her reached down and gripped her slender neck.

Naomi instantly realized what was happening. If this world *itself* was a simulation...then anything that wasn't present in the quantum records would be deleted. The Homeostatic System would destroy anything that didn't belong.

Ichigyou Ruri was a normal part of this world. But if the system detected her *consciousness*, her sixteen-year-old mind, as *something brought here from outside...*

Naomi could faintly hear her gasp as the thing's hands closed around her neck. She was going to be erased right in front of him. Those things were going to *kill* her.

"Stop!" he screamed wildly. "Stop it! Get off her, you bastard!"

The fox-mask ignored his cries. Its thick arms flexed as it pressed down on Ruri's neck.

She was going to die. There was nothing he could do to save her. He was just going to lie here on the floor and watch the woman he loved disappear forever.

This was what all his plans had come to.

"Katagaki...san..."

Her last, feeble words faded into silence.

"Aaah..."

His answer was a cry of absolute despair.

"Aaaaaaaaaaaaaagh!"

In that moment, Katagaki Naomi went completely mad.

A bizarre series of images streamed past his eyes. He saw Ruri being murdered, countless fox-masks, his city ripped apart and turned upside down.

He saw a hole that swallowed everything into its maw.

What? Wait. No. Is this...

He saw a shrine. A bird. A glove. A string. A rainbow tunnel.

Unfamiliar images spun through his mind...but *he* recognized them. They were memories of the past. Memories that belonged to a *different* Naomi.

Suddenly, his field of vision opened up again, and one final memory flashed before his eyes.

He was in Ruri's hospital room, and the fox-masks flew through the air.

From his spot on the floor, Naomi watched the masked thing that had been strangling Ruri get smashed against the far wall. Twenty others went soaring off in all directions, smashing hard into the ceiling and the walls.

They were pinned in place where they hit, bear traps materializing, clutching their limbs and holding them fast to the walls.

"Hcck! Haah!" Ruri coughed loudly and painfully, trying to catch her breath.

She was still alive.

Somehow, *Katagaki Naomi* was standing at her side.

2.

NAOMI LOOKED AROUND.

He'd taken care of all the fox-masks in the room itself, but there were still many of them in the hallway. The mass of bodies latched on to the window were still wriggling around like a ball of insects.

Naomi raised his right hand.

First, he waved a finger gently toward the hallway. A rainbow-colored crystalline wall rose up out of the floor, sealing the entrance shut.

Next, he raised his arm a little higher, then swept it to the side, as if wiping the dust off the top of a bookshelf. A wave of liquid crystal swept past outside the window, tossing the fox-masks away. The wave then solidified into another solid defensive wall.

He closed his hand into a fist, testing the feeling of the glove against his skin.

He hadn't been capable of anything like this before. He'd never managed to create something his glove wasn't touching, and summoning up objects this big had been an enormous strain on his mind.

But now, it wasn't a problem. He felt like he could do almost *anything.* With this new glove, he was ready to try some things he'd never risked doing before.

"Katagaki…san…"

He turned to face Ruri, and their eyes met. She was struggling to sit up in bed, wincing in pain.

He hurried over to her, reaching out with both hands. She reached out to him, too.

They ended up in each other's arms.

The warmth he felt was real. *She* was real. This was the first time he'd seen her at age twenty-six, and her body was painfully thin and fragile—it was clear how much of a toll those ten years in the coma had taken. But even that felt insignificant right now.

She was *here.*

He'd thought he would never see her again, but now he held her in his arms. She was alive and smiling. That was enough for him. He had to resist the urge to break down into tears right then and there.

He pulled back and looked her in the eyes. "Those masked things are after you specifically, Ichigyou-san."

"They are?"

"Yeah. But don't worry. I'll deal with them." Naomi squeezed her hand, trying to reassure her at least a little.

"Naomi…"

Naomi turned to see Sensei standing there.

He'd pulled himself up to his feet, using the windowsill and a nearby shelf to support his weight. He stared at Naomi in shock, like he'd just witnessed something *impossible.*

That was fair. It wasn't like Naomi had any idea how he'd gotten here, either.

Looking down, he spoke the one thing that might have some answers. "Could you come off for a second?" His glove slipped off his hand and transformed into a crow. He didn't need it for the moment—in fact, he wanted to be bare-handed.

Naomi walked over to Sensei and punched him in the face as hard as he could. With a grunt of pain, the man fell right back down to the floor.

Looking down at him, Naomi flapped his smarting hand in the air. He hadn't expected that to hurt so much. It had been worth it, though.

It feels a little weird to punch yourself.

Over the course of his journey here, when his memories merged with Sensei's, he saw *everything*. He *experienced* those ten long years like they were his own. He understood.

He understood far too well.

If I'd been in his shoes, I would have done the exact same thing.

It wouldn't have mattered how difficult or painful that path was, he would have followed it. He would give up his leg. He would give up his *whole life* for any chance to get her back. There was no doubt in his mind.

That was why he'd punched Sensei. The man would have done the same to him.

The crow returned to Naomi's hand and transformed back into his glove. With a small motion, Naomi opened a hole in the floor and created a simple escape chute to take them out of the hospital. Their destination went without saying.

He walked over to the bed and carefully took Ruri in his arms. He was a little nervous at first, but he managed to lift her without staggering.

Trying his very best not to let the strain show on his face, he smiled down at her. "Let's go back to where we belong."

Naomi carried Ruri to the escape chute, and they slid down together.

As quietly as he could, he asked the glove if it had any way to make the bridal-carry a little easier.

3.

IT WAS SUDDENLY VERY QUIET.

The hospital room that had been so frantic was almost empty. Katagaki Naomi had vanished as quickly as he appeared. Ichigyou Ruri, who'd spent the last ten years here, had gone with him. And the countless fox-masks had all disappeared, too.

There was only one person who still lingered here—a man with a bum leg and a bruise on his face, sitting quietly on the floor.

In the silence, Naomi was asking himself the hard questions.

What just happened?

How *did it happen?*

Where did I go so wrong?

Eventually, the shrill beeping of his cell phone brought him out of his reverie. The name *Senko Tsunehisa* appeared on the screen; he answered.

"Naomiiii!" There were shouts and frantic activity in the background of the call. "Where are you right now?!"

"The hospital."

"Well, take a look out the window!"

Picking up his cane, Naomi rose to his feet. The crystal structure that had covered the window earlier had disappeared when the *other* Katagaki Naomi left the area.

Opening the fourth-floor window, Naomi leaned out to look down at Kamanza Street. His breath caught in his throat.

There was a *river* running down the road. But it wasn't made of water; instead, it was a single enormous mass of humanoid bodies. There were tens of thousands of the fox-masks down there, flooding the streets completely.

It looked like the "river" was flowing south. Naomi looked in the opposite direction and soon found its source—the masked things were streaming out of the Chronicle Kyoto Project building, in other words, the AllTale Center.

"I see them."

"The AllTale's quantum-record bits are caught in a loop!" Senko shouted. The language was technical, but Naomi understood. "The amount of data in the system is multiplying rapidly—the logical boundary's been broken! I don't know what could have caused this, but it's *not* good!"

Naomi knew what had caused it. He was probably the only

person with enough information to know. He also knew what had to be done.

"Senko-san."

"Yeah?"

"Can you suspend the Homeostatic System?"

"What? No!" Senko protested. "I mean, these people with the fox masks are popping out of the room where it's housed—it won't respond to external commands at all, so we'd need to get rid of them first. And, I mean...you *know* it's not a good idea, Naomi."

There was a brief pause. When Senko continued, his voice was noticeably quieter.

"The Homeostatic System is AllTale's equivalent of a control rod. The only reason we can *use* the damn thing is because it's there, suppressing the quantum-record output to an absolute minimum. If we shut it down, well...uh..." Senko paused again, like he was thinking it over. "Wait. Seriously?" His voice returned to normal—it sounded like he'd arrived at the same conclusion.

"Its true capacity is infinite, if I recall," said Naomi.

"Heh heh, so it is! Now isn't *that* an idea. Let's give it a shot!"

"Please do. As for these fox-mask things...I'll deal with them somehow." Naomi spoke those words with all the conviction he could muster.

Ending the phone call, he reached out and grabbed hold of his cane.

4.

THE BICYCLE SPED DOWN Karasuma Street. Naomi pedaled in the front seat, with Ruri seated behind him, hanging on to his waist.

The bike moved along at a very decent clip, faster than even the average racing cycle could manage. Naomi had created it with his glove with speed in mind, so it worked like a souped-up e-bike with its speed limiter removed.

A motorcycle or car might've been faster choices, but just because he could *make* one of those didn't mean he knew how to *drive* them. The last thing he needed was to get them in an accident. The bike was the best option he could think of on the spur of the moment.

He guessed they were going about forty kilometers per hour, much faster than anyone, or anything, on foot could normally keep up with.

Unfortunately, their pursuers were far from *normal.*

Naomi shot a quick look over his shoulder. He could see a great mass of the fox-masks chasing after them, but they were pretty far behind. He was at least a little faster than them on this thing, so the gap was growing steadily.

A moment later, though, more masked things appeared out of nowhere just behind the bicycle. They lunged, and Naomi yanked the handlebars sharply to one side, heading for a side road—but a new group of fox-masks appeared there and lunged for them again.

They were starting to appear out of thin air now. That was new.

"The AllTale's region of influence is steadily expanding," explained his glove calmly. "In any region under its direct control, they can spawn at any coordinates."

"That's just *cheating*!" Naomi shouted, weaving his way around the newest group of enemies. Who ever heard of a game of tag where you were allowed to teleport on top of people?

Pedaling fiercely down the city's narrow side streets, he turned at every intersection he came to, avoiding the fox-masks as best he could. He'd been heading steadily down Karasuma Street at first, but they seemed to be herding him away from it at an angle.

Eventually, he found himself barreling toward a wide-open area—Horikawa-Gojo, a great swath of asphalt surrounded by a square pedestrian bridge.

Two major thoroughfares met here, one five lanes wide, the other six. This was one of Kyoto's single biggest intersections. On an ordinary afternoon, there should be dozens of cars crossing it constantly, but right now there wasn't a single one on the road.

There were, however, a truly massive number of fox-masks standing on the far side.

Naomi squeezed his handbrake with all his might, and the bicycle slid to a halt in the very center of the intersection. Turning in his seat, he looked around. The west, east, and south roads were all packed solid with walls of masked bodies. When he turned back to the north, he saw that the group pursuing him was closing in quickly.

There was nowhere left to run.

Naomi swallowed nervously and looked at the palm of his glove, hoping for some kind of hint. Was there any chance he could win this fight? He just didn't know.

Given his current capabilities, dispatching ten or twenty of these things wasn't much of a challenge. He felt confident he could take fifty at once, or even a hundred. But fifty *thousand*? A hundred thousand? He wasn't so sure about that.

He needed to keep Ruri safe no matter what. That made the situation considerably more dangerous. Even if he destroyed 99,999 of them, if a *single one* got through, that might be all it took. There was just no guarantee he'd catch every trick they pulled and wipe them out completely.

That was why he'd hoped to outrun the fox-masks and escape. Stopping to fight just meant more risk.

Naomi could feel his stomach clenching.

Ruri sat quietly behind him on the bicycle, her arms still wrapped around his chest. He didn't need to see her face to know that she was terrified.

Naomi squeezed his gloved hand into a fist. He had to do this. He'd destroy all 100,000 if he had to.

Just as he prepared to make his first attack, he heard a series of dull *thumps* in the distance. He turned toward the north side of the intersection as the sound grew louder.

Within the massive crowd of bodies, Naomi saw a bunch of them suddenly thrown into the air. Something was cutting directly through the fox-mask army, sending them flying as it went.

It broke free from the phalanx of fox-masks, and Naomi saw what it was—a car. The tires screeched loudly as it entered the intersection, and it came to a skidding halt just in front of Naomi's bicycle.

The driver's-side window slid open.

"Get in!"

Naomi froze just for a moment.

"Hurry up, damn it!"

Snapping out of his daze, Naomi quickly hopped down, took Ruri in his arms, and jumped into the back seat with her. The car accelerated fast, pressing them both against the leather.

Thump! Thump! Thump! Thump!

A series of dull impacts rocked the car, and dozens of fox-masks went flying by the windows. It was honestly a horrific sight. This wasn't something anyone could do if they thought those things were human.

Lucky for them, the driver knew they weren't.

"Sensei?" Naomi called tentatively from the back seat. He had so many questions on the tip of his tongue, but somehow they all fit inside one word.

Why?

Why was he here? Why was he helping them? Why should they *trust* him after what he'd done?

Why, Sensei?

"We'll take her back to the world where she belongs."

Naomi's eyes went wide. He wished he could see the look on

Sensei's face. He tried to see in the rearview mirror, but the angle was all wrong.

"It's my fault things turned out this way, you know?" Sensei continued, without any of the usual confidence in his voice. "This isn't what I wanted. I didn't want to put her through this. I just..." He paused, then spit out all at once, "I just wanted to see her smile again."

It was the same reason he'd given Naomi right after they'd met, up on the rooftop. The very same.

"I just want one smile."

"Just once, I want to see her really, truly happy."

He'd been telling the truth.

When he'd first said it, Naomi could only understand the surface meaning of his words. But now, he knew everything. He knew how *desperately* Sensei wanted to see that smile, and how much of himself he'd give up for a chance; he'd worked and plotted for ten whole years, burned his body and paralyzed his leg. And he'd never regretted it for a moment. There was nothing more precious to him in the entire world. *Nothing.* And he was going to *give it back*.

Not for his sake, of course. For *hers.* He wanted her to be happy.

"I'll make it up to you as best I can." Sensei turned back to look at them with his old focused, intense gaze. Those were the eyes of a man with no more doubts.

Naomi smiled.

"Just tell me where you want to go, Naomi!"

Naomi nodded. The crow on his hand had told him where to go next. It was the one place where the two of them could return to their own world. The final station, quite literally, where their three-month journey would reach its conclusion.

"The Grand Staircase at Kyoto Station!"

5.

LIGHT SHINED IN THROUGH the lattice of metal beams and glass panels that made up the main concourse at Kyoto Station. The ceiling of the main concourse was extremely high, with a large open space at its center—and that space opened up into the towering, broad steps of the famous Grand Staircase.

This massive staircase took people from the concourse all the way to the Sky Garden on the fifteenth floor, but it seemed much taller and grander than that, like it led straight to heaven. It was sixteen meters wide and over thirty meters tall, with a total of 171 steps. Many people found climbing the whole thing too challenging, so an escalator ran alongside it. If you looked up as you stepped onto these stairs, you'd see a dramatically arched glass roof and a long, suspended Skyway tunnel that hung diagonally in the air above you. It looked more like a movie set than an ordinary train station.

A car skidded to a halt in the Sky Garden at its summit, seventy meters above the ground.

The sightseers in the main concourse stared up at it, wide-eyed in shock. The *ramp* this car had driven up, which appeared to be made of rainbow-colored crystal, melted before their eyes into particles of light.

The onlookers were still frozen in shock when the car's doors swung open.

"We're here!"

Katagaki Naomi leapt out of the back seat, followed closely by Sensei and Ruri. Ruri was moving slowly, even slower than Sensei despite his disability—the years she'd spent unconscious had weakened her body severely.

Sensei saw her struggling and started to reach out to her, but he made himself stop. He couldn't let himself touch her. He needed to keep his distance.

He had no right to go anywhere near her.

"So, what are we doing here?" he asked, turning to Naomi, but the boy was busy talking to his glove. Sensei didn't know what the deal was with this new crow—the one *he'd* created hadn't been able to talk.

"We must make some preparations," the glove said, its tone calm. "Please clear the area."

"What?" Naomi said. "How am I supposed to do that?"

"Use your hand."

A bit uncertainly, Naomi pressed his hand to the ground in front of the staircase.

There was a railing running down the center of the stairs—the top of it bulged up out of the floor, creating strange balloons that covered the stairs to either side in a wall that traveled downward. It grew slowly larger, forming a speckled yellow-black barrier that looked almost alive.

The people on the stairs scurried down in panic at the bizarre sight; those who didn't escape in time were pushed along and deposited gently at the bottom.

When the staircase was completely covered in the odd, spotted balloons, they swelled up in unison and burst, then faded away into nothingness. In the aftermath of this magic trick, the Grand Staircase was left totally deserted.

"Converter," Naomi's glove chirped. A flash of light ran from his hand across the ground, and something new took shape on the first stair leading downward.

It wasn't immediately clear what it was—a large, geometrical object slowly pieced itself together out of colored triangles that looked like stained glass. As it came together, the surreal spectacle arranged itself into the familiar shape of an arched doorway.

"We'll make these at regular intervals on the entire staircase," the glove explained helpfully. "With each one that Ichigyou Ruri passes through, her quantum conversion will progress slightly. When she reaches the bottom of the staircase, the quantization process will be complete, and she can return to her original world."

Sensei listened closely, his mind running at full speed. The technique this thing was describing sounded much more advanced than the method he'd used to enter AllTale's quantum-record world. He could barely follow it.

"We will convert Ichigyou Ruri first," the glove continued, "then Katagaki Naomi."

Sensei turned to look at Ruri. She was trembling, and not just because of her physical condition.

There were *171 steps* on this staircase.

It was the equivalent of ten flights of stairs. Even a perfectly healthy person might hesitate at the sight of that descent; in her weakened state, she couldn't possibly walk down these stairs alone. She needed someone to help her or she'd never make it, but Naomi would be busy creating the doorways.

Could he help her somehow?

"Don't worry, Ichigyou-san," said Naomi, his tone almost cheerful. "You can do this. Just take it nice and slow, one step at a time."

Ruri nodded seriously. With visible effort of will, she stopped her hands from trembling. She took a deep breath and clutched them into fists.

"Let's do this," she said at last.

At that instant, Sensei finally understood. These two were *different*. Naomi wasn't him, and this girl wasn't the Ruri he had known.

His mind was pulled back to decade-old memories.

That fire had destroyed *all* the books they'd gathered. Ruri had been heartbroken, and he'd tried his best to comfort her. They'd learned, together, the pain of accepting failure. And in enduring it together, they'd grown closer.

But these two were different.

Their books had burned as well, but they'd seen that as a *challenge*. They'd thrown themselves at it, and they'd overcome it. They'd made the book sale a success. And that moment of triumph had changed them both.

Sensei chuckled softly, derisively, at himself. He'd intended to make it up to them as best he could, but he clearly wasn't good for much. His only use so far was his driving skills.

Well, so be it. That's fine by me.

"Please hurry," the talking glove chirped. "The system's area of influence will reach this location shortly."

With a quick nod, Naomi hurried down the stairs and began creating the second door, then a third and a fourth, each as colorful as the last. The path was growing, bit by bit.

As he worked, the first door opened invitingly.

"Go ahead," the glove called from below.

Apparently this "conversion" process was already starting, even though the doors themselves were still a work in progress. Naomi had just finished off his sixth; it brought him past the first landing.

Ruri stood in front of the first door. Screwing up her courage, maybe?

"Get moving," Sensei said as coldly as he could manage. "You need to hurry." It felt cruel to speak to her that way, but they didn't have much time to waste. Someone had to push her forward.

For some reason, though, she paused to look at him. There was a familiar strength in her eyes—it didn't *look* like she was hesitating out of fear.

"What's wrong?"

"Are you Katagaki-san?" she asked him quietly.

Sensei's eyes went wide. It wasn't a question he'd expected, but he could certainly understand why she might be confused. Unlike he and Naomi, there was a lot she didn't understand yet. She didn't know her world was a simulation, or how the two of them were connected.

But at this point, she didn't need to know the whole truth. She understood the things that *mattered.*

"No," Sensei replied.

He looked over at the stairs. Naomi was still hard at work, frantically creating one door after another.

"That's Katagaki Naomi over there."

And I...

"I'm just a minor character."

I'm not Katagaki Naomi anymore. He's *the protagonist of this story.*

"Go on, now." He urged her on once again, reaching out to gently push her forward.

Instead, she turned around and embraced him.

It was so sudden. His mind went blank; all he could manage was staring stupidly down at the top of her head. Her arms were wrapped all the way around him, squeezing gently.

She said something, mumbling into his chest.

"You did love me, didn't you?"

The words sank in slowly, permeating his empty mind. She didn't know anything. She wasn't *supposed* to know anything.

She'd fallen unconscious at age sixteen, then woken up suddenly only a few days ago. There was no possible way she could know about the real nature of this world, or the events of the last decade, or the reasons he'd lied.

And yet, she'd cut right through it all and found the one essential truth under the countless lies.

Ruri separated her hands and pulled back slowly. She looked up at him with a smile on her face.

"Thank you."

There was strength in her eyes. Turning, she took her first step forward.

"And goodbye!"

She passed through the first door. It *interacted* with her, and the boundary between her body and the world grew less distinct. The lines of her physical form seemed a little blurrier; a small part of her was reduced to particles of light, which faded quickly into the air.

She was leaving this world.

"Ichigyou-san..." Sensei replied, his words too quiet to reach her, "you're right."

She was going to disappear. He was never going to see her again.

The tears running down his face were the only thing that made it feel real.

"I..."

As she faded into the light, Sensei spoke his final words to her. For once, they were the whole, simple truth.

"I loved you so, *so* much."

6.

"It's done!"

The final door pieced itself together. The moment it was complete, it swung open to accept a mysterious stream of light that flowed into it from above.

The glove had told him what it was—Ruri, now converted into quantum particles.

"Naomi!" Sensei shouted from above. "It's your turn now! Get a move on!"

"Right!"

Naomi ran up the stairs as fast as he could. Ruri's conversion had gone more quickly than he expected; at this rate, he might be able to follow her before the fox-masks showed up inside the station.

But just as he let himself think it could be an easy victory, something above him moved alarmingly.

"Wha..."

The Skyway, the large tunnel walkway suspended high above the Grand Staircase, creaked dangerously. A moment later, it started to fall—right on top of Naomi and his gateways.

Naomi swung his glove up on sheer reflex, summoning a crude crystal roof some distance above him. But the Skyway was just too massive; when it struck the roof, both were smashed to pieces, sending countless chunks of rubble right down at him.

He swung his glove again, as forcefully as he could. A long crystalline rod extended from his hand like the Monkey King's staff, launching Naomi into the air as it hit the floor. He flew clear of the rubble a split second before it rained down on the staircase.

Naomi hit the ground of the Sky Garden hard, tumbling backward until Sensei stopped him.

Sensei stared down at the staircase and the clouds of dust rising from it with a grimace. Naomi turned to follow his gaze and made the same face.

The Grand Staircase had been crushed.

Most of its surface was buried under broken remnants of the Skyway and the glass roof above it. The steps that had been hit directly were completely destroyed, and the rest was buried under a huge mound of rubble.

The series of doors that Naomi had just created had disappeared under gray chunks of concrete.

"Oh no..."

Naomi stared down at the destruction, overwhelmed with anguish. He could see now just what had happened—there was a yawning hole in the north wall of the station, and a giant ball, several meters across, was embedded in the southern wall.

The surface of the ball was pulsing in a strange, nauseating way, and after a moment, Naomi realized it was entirely made up of fox-masked figures. Dozens of them had clumped together tightly to form an enormous bullet, which had struck the station and destroyed the Skyway.

As Naomi watched, another thought occurred to him—if that thing was a bullet, something must have *fired* it.

Naomi and Sensei both turned to the north. From their

viewpoint on the Sky Garden, the two of them looked out at the city, past Kyoto Tower and beyond.

First, they saw what looked like a bizarre string—thick, white and massive, taller than Kyoto Tower—undulating in the distance. The next moment, more of them rose up one by one, wriggling like worms as they grew steadily taller, until there were nine great squirming strings.

It was only then that Naomi realized they were the *tails* of an enormous animal. The body of the thing came into view, white with black stripes and clearly made of the same stuff as the "bullet" embedded in the station's wall... So, a colossal monster made up of the fox-masks.

"Monster" was the only term that felt appropriate. It walked through the city like a living thing, but it was taller than Kyoto Tower. Its arms, or forelegs, grabbed the buildings in its path like they were toy blocks.

It looked like a fox forcing itself to walk on two legs, or maybe a human trying to walk on all fours. It looked *wrong*. It didn't belong in this world.

Naomi exhaled sharply. His mind, which had shut down from shock, finally started working again.

"Sensei, are you—"

"I'm fine."

They were both uninjured, at least. They each gave the other a quick look, then turned back to the enormous monster.

"We've got to do something about that thing..."

Naomi looked down at his glove and focused as hard as he

could. He needed to create something that could get rid of that behemoth.

For some reason, that was as far as his train of thought would carry him.

Uh...how am I supposed to do that?!

His thoughts ran in circles, but his overwhelmed, panicky mind couldn't come up with a plan that could work. The God Hand could do *anything*, in theory. Anything he could imagine would become real in this world. He *knew* that.

Only problem was, his imagination couldn't keep up with *this*.

Suddenly, the world grew dark as a shadow was cast over the area. Naomi and Sensei jerked their heads up toward the sky.

The top of Kyoto Tower was tumbling through the air straight at them.

"Aaaaaah!"

Naomi swung his hand into the air reflexively, unsure what he was even trying to create. An odd, stringy crystal beam shot up off the ground and hit the tower's observation deck, catching it in midair. But it wasn't enough to hold it there for long; the deck's enormous weight bore down on the structure and it began to crumble away.

Naomi threw another support beam at the deck, then another and another in quick succession, fighting to halt its fall. In the end, he just barely got the upper hand—the observation deck came to a halt directly above the Sky Garden. It was a surreal spectacle, but Naomi couldn't step back to admire it. It took all concentration just to keep the thing where it was.

This is insane. This is insane!

"Naomi!" Sensei shouted from behind him.

Naomi knew they were in trouble the moment he heard that cry. An instant later, the shadow they stood in turned even darker.

Above the suspended observation deck, a foreleg even larger than the top of the tower swung down.

The colossal leg stepped down onto the very top of the broken Kyoto Tower, forcing it downward with impossible force. Naomi's support beams shuddered.

"Gaaah!"

He fought back with *everything* he had. His glove groaned with exertion as it brought forth more and more support beams every second. Naomi's head burned with exhaustion, a sensation he hadn't felt yet with this new glove. It reminded him of his training sessions, and of creating that black hole on the bridge.

His brain was reaching its limit.

But he couldn't let up now. If he flinched, it would all be over. That enormous leg would crush him and Sensei into paste in an instant.

He had to do this, but he *couldn't*. Those two conflicting facts filled his brain; pure blackness spread across his mind like a pool of ink.

Oh crap. Oh God. Somebody, please—

"Naomi," said Sensei, "we're going to beat that thing."

A ray of light cut through the blackness.

Naomi looked over his shoulder. Sensei was still sitting on

the ground, unable to rise, his cane lost somewhere in the chaos. But he had a bold smile on his face. He was suddenly the fearless, cocky man Naomi had spent so much time with back in his world.

If Sensei said they were going to take that monster down, it was all going to be fine. Sensei knew just what to do—he always had the perfect idea ready and waiting.

He was Naomi's *Sensei*, after all.

"Use the God Hand to erase me," Sensei said, "right now."

"What?"

Naomi stopped. *I don't get it,* he told himself. *That doesn't make sense.* He tried to convince himself that was true, violently suppressed the part of him that understood.

"You don't need me to explain, do you?"

"But that's...that's just..." No matter how hard he tried to push it down, the truth wormed its way back into his mind.

He didn't *want* to understand, but he knew exactly what Sensei was thinking. The fox-masks had been after Ichigyou Ruri. They had wanted to erase her because they'd identified her as a *foreign object,* something alien to this world.

But now that she'd left it, the masked things were clearly targeting *them.*

"The System's highest-priority repair operation is the elimination of duplicate addresses," Sensei began, explaining the technical aspect on purpose to give Naomi the necessary background. "Any duplicate records have to be trimmed. Two versions of the same object can't coexist in a single world. In other words..."

Sensei pointed at Naomi. "Once one of *us* is erased, those things will stop."

And then, he pointed at himself.

"The answer should be obvious."

"No. No way!" Naomi shouted. He wouldn't accept this—it was just too horrible. He needed another solution.

Maybe he could just recreate that line of doors. He could go back home, and Sensei wouldn't be a duplicate anymore. That made sense, right? He just had to take this big thing down first.

"It'll be all right. I can do this!" Naomi focused his mind and forced more power out of his glove.

Sweat was dripping down his face.

"I'll just take this thing down real quick."

He forced *more* power out. The veins in his arm bulged with the strain. Something fell to the ground with a small *plip*—it was blood, dripping from his nose.

"Then I'll make that Converter again, and—"

"Naomi."

"I won't do it!" he shouted, more fiercely than before. How many times did he have to repeat himself? He was kind of busy at the moment, he didn't have time for irrelevant arguments.

But irrelevant *thoughts* just kept coming.

"I know what you're thinking... You want a girlfriend."

"You and Ichigyou Ruri will be dating three months from today."

"You can call me Sensei, then."

"Your romance is just getting started."

"Tell yourself you're a wizard from a fantasy novel."

"You're going to do the same."

"Don't be an idiot!"

"I'll give that a passing grade."

"I know you, Naomi."

"You can do this."

Tears streamed down Naomi's face. Three months' worth of memories played on a loop inside his head, the three months they'd spent together, working toward the same goal.

"I won't do it..."

He couldn't stop crying. His face was a total mess, but there was still strength in his arms. He remembered everything Sensei had taught him.

"You're the one who told me I can do anything, Sensei! You're the one who taught me to *believe* I can!"

He'd turned back to look Sensei in the eyes and scream his heart out, "I'm going to beat this thing! We're *both* going to survive!"

"Nao—"

Sensei's voice cut off abruptly. Naomi turned back, following his gaze into the sky.

Suddenly, there were small flashes somewhere very far away, and *something* headed toward him almost faster than his eyes could follow. He couldn't tell what it was at first, but then he recognized it as the fox-monster's nine "tails," all rushing right toward him.

In less than a second, they were going to pierce right through him, and he was going to die. He didn't have time to move—

Blood splattered into the air, confirming his death. More and more rained down to the ground like water pouring from an open faucet. But something was wrong...Naomi raised his head.

Sensei was in standing of him. All nine tails had skewered him.

He had shielded Naomi with his body.

"Ah..." Naomi shook his head. "Aah..." He didn't understand. *How* was Sensei standing there? How had he even gotten to his feet?

"It's...true," Sensei said, smiling that familiar fearless smile. "You can do anything...you believe you can."

He gave Naomi one more lesson. Like a mentor. Like a teacher.

"Sensei..." Naomi called out his title. "Sensei!" It was all he could think of to do, even if, in that moment, he felt like the world's most useless, incompetent student.

His teacher reached out his trembling right hand. Naomi understood. He wasn't much of a pupil, but he knew how to respond to this, at least.

He took Sensei's hand in his own and squeezed it tightly.

This was a ritual, the same one they'd performed at the very beginning. It was an echo of the promise they'd made each other on that rooftop, all those months ago.

Back then, they hadn't been able to touch each other, so they'd gone through the motions awkwardly, as a formality. But now, at long last...Naomi could take his hand.

Through that hand, *everything* flowed into him. Sensei's feelings were his own. For just a moment, they were a single person, with a single answer.

This was the end.

"Katagaki..." Sensei choked out, "Naomi." He spoke his pupil's name, one last time, then he smiled more gently than he ever had before.

"Go live a happy life."

Naomi simply squeezed his hand. They'd made their decision, together.

His glove let out a burst of brilliant rainbow light and opened the path that led to God.

For the first time, he could feel the boy's warmth against his hand. Even through the glove, he could still feel it clearly. He idly thought that maybe the kid's body temperature was higher than his, but that didn't make much sense, did it?

His body grew lighter. The pain had disappeared; he was breathing much easier now. It was a big relief. His only real regret was that he couldn't say thanks.

He didn't fight the feeling—he just relaxed and let it wash over him. The power coursing into him through his right hand spread across his body and out his back. He couldn't see it happening, but he was probably vanishing from back to front.

He had a little time before his head disappeared, then. Not much, but a little. He used it to reminisce.

He saw her face.

Memories from ten years ago flitted through his mind. He'd told her how he felt a few weeks after the fire. When she agreed to go out with him, he'd nearly passed out on the spot.

He'd always been an indecisive person. But for the first time, he chose someone.

On the day of her accident, he'd lost his future. She was the only one for him. She was *everything* to him. And so, he'd vowed to do whatever it took to get her back.

He'd vowed to make a future for both of them.

Yes...for *both of them.*

"I read it there every month, too."

"I'm not good with heights."

"Let's do everything we can."

"Are you Katagaki-san?"

"You did love me, didn't you?"

"Uh, not really..."

"If that's all true, why are you here?"

"So what am I supposed to call you, anyway? I mean, you're me."

"What was excellent about that?!"

"But right now, she's miserable."

"Thank you so much!"

"I won't do it!"

"We're both going to survive!"

"Sensei..."

"Sensei?"

He let himself imagine their future. And at the very end, he murmured to himself, "I'm a happy man."

The words faded into light...and he disappeared into the heavens.

7.

THE FOX-MASKS BROKE APART and disappeared.

It barely took any time at all. The masked things abruptly stopped moving, then dissolved into dust; the particles quickly grew smaller, then vanished without a trace.

The world's mass decreased as the weight and volume of thousands upon thousands of real, physical bodies disappeared like they had never existed in the first place.

The first thought that passed through Senko Tsunehisa's mind was that it would probably take way too much time and effort to develop any coherent, logical explanation for this phenomenon. But as long as he didn't have to *explain* it, he already had a pretty good idea of what had happened.

It was a half-baked theory, but it was good enough for him. There was probably one other person out there who'd believe it, too.

The kid had said he was going to *deal with them* somehow. And somehow, they'd been dealt with. This was probably his doing. Now it was Senko's turn to keep his side of the bargain.

Barging into the chamber, which he could finally reach with the fox-masks gone, he rushed over to the Homeostatic System's control panel and threw open the steel door. His eyes found the large metal switch connected to the emergency shutdown relay.

Once this thing was flipped, AllTale would immediately spring into action. The infinite-capacity quantum computer he had created would unleash its *real* power for the very first time.

But once it did so, it would move beyond his control forever. No human being would ever be able to domesticate it again. Even the laws of nature might no longer bind it.

There was no telling what might happen after that; the consequences would be utterly unpredictable. He couldn't even guess what wonders or horrors might ensue.

In other words, flipping this switch wasn't exactly a *responsible* decision.

Senko reached out to grab it anyway.

Maybe this is what God felt like on the first day.

8.

THE ENORMOUS FOX MONSTER broke apart.

The individual bodies that had formed the colossus began to fall away from it, tumbling down toward the streets outside Kyoto Station. But before they could strike the ground, they melted into nothingness. It looked a bit like cherry blossoms falling in a gust of wind.

The creature's forearm faded away, and the enormous pressure bearing down on Naomi disappeared. His crystal support beams wrapped themselves around Kyoto Tower's observation deck and lowered it gently to the ground.

He could use his power freely now. There was nothing left to hold him back.

But his hand was empty.

"Katagaki Naomi-san," his glove called out to him.

His right hand rose up on its own; the entire surface of the glove was now a rainbow of colors. Its glow, faint at first, grew steadily brighter. The light engulfed Naomi, then the Sky Garden, then the entire station.

In the distance, he could see something similar happening. There was a faint dome of light spreading out to the north, centered somewhere between Nijo Castle and the Imperial Palace. He couldn't be sure, but he thought it was coming from the AllTale Center.

The two domes grew steadily larger and larger, until finally, somewhere near Shijo Street, they made contact.

In that moment—

A world was created.

□

Naomi was there.

There was Naomi.

There was nothing, but also everything.

There was *one* and *zero*. All and naught. Yes and no.

At first, they were intermingled, but soon they sorted

themselves out. Once distinct, they began to grow, expanding ferociously.

There was space and time. There were stars and living things. There were people and their cities. There was heaven and hell. There were books and stories.

There was everything. And yet, more kept coming. More and more and more. The growth seemed endless.

As infinity stretched out before him, Naomi took a piece of it in his hands.

It was Sensei's notebook, the *Ultimate Manual.*

He recognized it by its cover. But when he looked more closely, he saw it was brand new. There was no title written on it yet.

Naomi flipped through it for a moment.

It was no great surprise, really...but all the pages were blank.

■

He heard the sound of a train in the distance.

The air was crisp and clear and felt like morning. That train was probably the first of the day, or maybe the second.

Fluffy white summer clouds drifted by slowly overhead. The sky above the mountains was vivid blue. And a familiar tower stood tall above the city, intact and unharmed.

He was in Kyoto.

He looked around uncertainly. He was standing in the exact same place he last remembered being—at the top of Kyoto

Station's Grand Staircase, in the Sky Garden, with its scenic view of the entire city. It was still early in the morning, so the area was deserted.

There was only one other person there. She was standing at the center of the garden, amidst its concrete and greenery.

It was *her.*

"Katagaki-san?" she called.

"Ichigyou-san!"

They ran toward each other and embraced.

After a moment, they pulled back for a second look—to make sure that this was real.

The girl *was* Ichigyou Ruri. The boy *was* Katagaki Naomi. They were both sixteen years old, just as they'd been when they were torn apart.

They were both alive, and they wouldn't be parted again.

Somehow, instinctively, Naomi knew this. He knew they could be together from now on. But he still couldn't stop himself from squeezing her tightly in his arms. In fact, a hug wasn't enough to satisfy him—he grabbed her hand, too.

His hand was sweaty, unfortunately. But so was hers. Their palms pressed together, exchanging heat.

He didn't have the glove on anymore.

Together, they looked out at Kyoto, hand in hand. It was a brilliant, sunny morning, and the city lay unchanged before their eyes, as beautiful as ever.

"Did we...?"

Ruri's voice trailed off, her question only halfway spoken.

Did we make it back to our world?

She still didn't know enough to clearly understand what had happened, but some part of her instinctually knew.

It wasn't like Naomi really understood much of anything himself. He couldn't explain what had just happened, and he didn't have any clear answers about what this place was. Even if he did come up with something, there was no one who could confirm he was right.

In the "real world," answers didn't come with a guarantee. In other words...the next thing he said might be true, or might not.

"I think—"

Naomi put his pen to this blank, white world. Facing an empty page where he could write anything he pleased, he chose the first line all by himself.

"I think this is a brand-new world. One that no one knows about."

In this new world, they could do anything they wanted. Nothing was destined. Nothing was preordained.

But he already knew what he *wanted* to do.

He was going to live a happy life.

"C'mon, kid. You're just following my orders again?"

Naomi answered the small voice in his head silently, but with real pride.

Actually, I made my own decision this time.

HELLO WORLD
THE NOVEL

EPILOGUE

KATAGAKI NAOMI opened his eyes.

The first thing he saw was a stark white ceiling. It looked like one you'd find in a laboratory, or maybe a hospital.

"The contents needed to fit their vessel perfectly."

A woman was speaking to him in a steady voice that reminded him of a voicemail menu. He recognized it immediately—it was the same voice he'd heard from the boy's glove.

His foggy, sluggish thoughts turned back to those final moments. He remembered the one thing he'd been worried about at the very end.

Did the kid get a happy ending, or what?

"You gave everything you had to save the people you loved. As a result, we were finally able to synchronize your consciousness with its vessel."

The words slowly percolated through his mind. Gradually, his eyes and thoughts grew more focused.

He was lying in a bed, and there was someone standing next to it. There was some kind of machinery behind her.

The woman looked a bit different from the girl he'd known.

He still recognized her instantly. She was the person he loved more than any other, after all.

"Katagaki-san..."

She was smiling. That smile had always been his greatest treasure.

"We *did* it."

Tears rolling freely down her face, Ichigyou Ruri dropped down and threw her arms around Naomi.

He reached out, his hands trembling weakly. His arms were terribly thin, and it was hard to move.

He had no idea how many years had passed. But that didn't matter. Not even a little. Slowly, carefully, he wrapped his arms around the girl he'd never expected to see again.

The vast, empty pages of a new world quietly awaited his next line.

HELLO WORLD
THE NOVEL